R A

THE GUEST

Mitali Meelan

Black Ink

Published by:
Black Ink
E 4/15, 4th Floor
Krishna Nagar, New Delhi 110051
E-mail: queries@blackinkbooks.in
Website: www.BlackInkBooks.in

First published by Black Ink in India in 2016

ISBN 13: 9788192982229

Typeset at Arpit Printographers, Delhi
Printed at Yash Printographics, Noida

For Daji, our four-pawed furry child. You showered us with joy, laughter and madness and drenched us in your love. You'll forever be alive in our memories and our hearts.

Chapter One

'This is Cecelia.' My father introduces his colleague to me while hauling her bags inside the house. Two large American Touristers block our entrance.

Cecelia smiles at him. 'Thank you, Mr Ranade. You shouldn't have,' she says. Dad waves his hand dismissively and they both turn to look at me. Keeping her smile intact, Cecelia extends a hand.

I hesitate. Dad narrows his eyes behind her, mouthing, 'Take it.' I slip my hand into hers and pull away after a quick shake.

'She'll be staying here for a month. I will be in the office mostly. So it's your responsibility to take care of her,' he says for the umpteenth time and walks around Cecelia to pat my shoulder. He gives her an encouraging smile. 'She'll guide you through now. I've to get back to work if you don't mind.'

'Oh, sure,' she says in her heavily accented voice. Her fair complexion is reddened by the Mumbai heat. Her short brunette hair falls along her heart-shaped face and her long, pointed nose gives her otherwise soft features an edge. She wears a loose beige top that falls over her black leggings. She isn't exactly fat, but more tall and curvy.

'Feel at home,' Dad says before walking out of the room.

When he leaves, an awkward silence lingers between the two of us. The room fills with the strong fragrance of rose perfume that overpowers Dad's musk scented aftershave that I'm so used to. It's an unsettling feeling.

Cecelia politely looks around the living room where we stand, checking it out—the paintings, the bookshelf, the ceiling. It's not very fancy, just like any other room in this house, but it's more than enough for two people. An empty bookshelf over a television, a few paintings scattered across white walls and a contrasting green sofa set in the middle is pretty much all there is. The only thing worth noticing is the balcony attached to it. If you stand there you can see the back of our garden and hear traffic bustling in the late evenings.

Cecelia's body remains still while her eyes travel and along with them, comes her approval. Going by her look, she seems impressed.

'Nice house.' Her eyes finally rest on me and crinkle with warmth. I force a smile back at her.

* * *

Two days ago, Dad announced the news that one of his colleagues, Cecelia Barnes was coming to India for some work. She'd stay with us for little more than a month before heading back. I was indifferent to the idea, but when he said I'd be the only one with her all day and she knew no one else in India, I stomped my foot down hard and protested.

A guest was okay, but Dad should have to look after her since she was *his* colleague and therefore, *his* guest. The thought that I'd have to live with a person completely unknown to me, entertain her every now and then and make sure she was comfortable for as long as a month freaked me out. It wasn't something I was used to. I explained this to him.

'Well,' he said that night, avoiding eye contact, 'she wasn't the one who said she wanted to live with us. I invited her.'

'Why?'

He put aside the egg beater and added salt, onion and chili powder to the bowl. He slowly poured the mixture into the pan, now testing my patience. When he looked pleased with the way it spread, he said, 'When I was in Canada for three years, I left you here with your nani. Cecelia was one of my subordinates and she made sure I felt at home. She showed me around the country and helped me digest the cultural shock. So I am obliged to do the same for her now.'

Of course, he was obliged, but then he should have stayed at home and fulfilled his obligations. Why throw this responsibility at me?

'And I invited her out of politeness,' he added. 'Now it's not my fault that she accepted it. I just asked her, like once, and she said she wouldn't mind a little vacation.'

I snorted. Vacations are always fun for the person who decides to take one, but a nightmare for the host, especially when you barge into someone's house knowing they'll be busy. 'We have a facility for people like her, you know,' I said. 'It's called a hotel.'

'I can't send her to a hotel when I live in the city!' he exclaimed, tapping the spatula on the pan a little too forcefully. Then, he sighed, 'A month, two months, how does it matter? And now that she's coming, we don't have a choice, do we? Have a heart, hon. What is your problem?'

I groaned. 'I don't mind her coming, not too much anyway. What I mind is that I'll be stuck with her all day when I'll have important stuff to do in college. And I'm sure you'll ask me to "show her around" Mumbai to keep her amused.'

Dad turned from the stove, made a sad face and switched to a tone that was meant to emotionally blackmail me, knowing that would melt my heart. 'Can't you do this one thing for Daddy?' I shook my head vehemently. 'What kind of a daughter are you!' he said in mock indignation. I crossed my hands over my chest. I wasn't going to budge—not this time.

Dad sighed and met my eyes with a final I'm-the-Dad-and-I'll-have-the-last-word look. It was rare, but when he gave me that look, I had no other option but to oblige.

'She's coming—like either of us has a choice anyway—and staying here with us. And your duty, as a daughter and a good person, is to take care of her.' Seeing my expression, his tone softened. 'Neha, it's only for a month, *beta*. Why is it so difficult? You can even be friends with her. She has got interesting foreign stories to share. You can tell her about your college. Don't look at it as if it's going to be a prison sentence. Try to enjoy her visit.'

I knew I was fighting a losing battle, so I decided to let it rest. One thing that was good about agreeing to it was that Dad seemed happy. And his happiness meant the world to me. Besides, the sight and aroma of those hot, steaming eggs made my stomach rumble. I was too hungry to fight anyway.

* * *

'Nay-ha,' Cecelia calls me, nudging my shoulder. Realizing she has been saying something to me, I bring my wandering mind back to the room and look up at her. 'May I use your washroom?' she asks.

I nod. Then I realize she is new to the place and doesn't know where to look for one. Not bothering to appear polite or welcoming, I tell her to follow me, wondering how I'd deal with this awkwardness for the whole month.

I also wonder what I'll need to do for her next… cook lunch maybe? Or she'll just ask me to order something from a restaurant. I doubt she can cook Indian meals, or cook any meal for that matter. She doesn't come across as a person who would stay indoors and concoct meals for families.

When I show her to the washroom, she puts a hand on the door knob and turns to face me. 'Don't worry, Nay-ha. I am not a pushy guest. I won't demand your time or expect you to keep me amused all the time. You're free to act the way you want, even when I'm around. So, cheer up.' She smiles and closes the door behind her.

I arch a brow at the closed door. I have never met an aunt who's asked me to cheer up. In fact, I'm always the one who says such things to older people.

Maybe Cecelia is different, I hope distantly. Maybe I'll survive this month after all.

'And I'm easy to please. Just a smile will do it.' Her voice, loud and friendly, comes from inside the washroom, while I try to shrug off the uneasiness I felt at her arrival. I look at the closed door for a second and smile. For the first time in the past couple of days, I find my shoulders relaxing.

Chapter Two

I let the two older people freshen up and stroll into the kitchen. I know Dad didn't cook anything in the morning. He woke up at around five and set off to pick Cecelia up from Mumbai Airport with two of his friends, Bob Uncle and Geeta Aunty. Her flight was delayed for about an hour, so they had to wait till 10:30 to finally get home. Good for me, though. I didn't have to give up on my sleep to greet her.

But in all the hustle, Dad hadn't found time to cook breakfast or lunch, which he usually did in the morning. And now the clock strikes twelve, time for him to rush to office.

I open the refrigerator door to check if there is anything left from last night's dinner. There is some *paneer*, *dal* and rice. There are also a few *rotis*, enough for the two of us. *I mean the three of us*, I correct myself.

Has Cecelia ever tasted Indian food before? Will she even like all this? She did say she wouldn't bother me for anything, so she might as well eat whatever I put on her plate.

Something soft and fluffy rushes past my feet and I glance down to find Rocky, my pet Labrador, hanging out in his favourite spot. Whenever we have something cooking in the kitchen, he almost always finds a way to reach it, his best trick—wagging his tail at the cook with his tongue hanging out. The patented puppy face works every time. I grab a biscuit and shove it into his mouth.

He is the first love of my life and seeing as how guys can be a pain in the arse, my last too. One good thing about dogs is that they are awfully loyal. My dog doesn't flirt with my girlfriends. He is happy to simply see me show up at the door every day. He is not demanding or self-centred and he wouldn't reprimand me for trivial slip-ups. He is in every way better than my boyfriend. No wonder Darshak hates him.

Rocky inhales his biscuit before I can straighten up in my seat and he blinks at me. Damn him! Patting the top of his head and fondling his ears, I order him to wait till his lunch is ready. He has grown far too stout for his age given the normal size of his breed.

He licks my hand and sits in a corner to gnaw his rubber bone without a hint of a grudge against me. He is a sweetheart. Apart from the only hitch that he is always hungry, Rocky is an otherwise unspoiled dog. There is not a single mean bone in his body. He is so full of love and void of any lust that I wish boys were like him.

I mentioned this to Darshak while we devoured South Indian food in our canteen one day. 'He lives with humans, Neha. Let him out in the presence of female dogs and see him change his colours,' Darshak had said, pointing his spoon at me and smiling through a mouthful of food. 'Or rather adhere to his true colours.'

I punched his arm, muttering that at least Rocky was pleased to see me come home every day. He jumped and licked me all over to show his joy. That was the beauty of his loyalty.

Darshak simply shrugged, his lips curving to form a smile. 'If that's what you want, then I don't mind jumping all over you to show how happy I am.'

He laughed. I pushed the piece of *dosa* between his fingers into his mouth. He had to cover his mouth to keep it all in. I chuckled before passing him a glass of water.

* * *

Two fingers snap in front of my eyes. 'Where are you lost?'

I find Dad towering over me and I'm back in the kitchen. Cecelia stands at the entrance looking amused.

'Nowhere,' I say, busying my hands with setting the food to heat on the stove. Dad stares at me with an odd, piercing look, like he can read my mind and doesn't like what he's reading.

Cecelia, on the other hand, tilts her head to the side, like everything she sets her eyes on amuses her; or, like she is about to enjoy a father-daughter fight. Whatever the reason, I fight a sudden urge to wipe the smile off her face.

Dad peeks inside a few containers and blinks up at me. 'Are you going to reheat what we had yesterday and offer it to our guest?'

I shrug indifferently. 'I can cook a very limited number of dishes. And this,' I nod at the food, 'is good and edible. She won't be poisoned.'

I want to let her know that my dad might pamper her as a guest, but that I won't. He crosses his arms over his protruding belly, his moustache newly trimmed. He smells of everything corporate. That look he tries to give me isn't scary at all, if he means it to be.

'Limited means ready-to-cook meals and omelette.' He frowns.

'You forgot brewing tea.'

'Neha…' As Dad starts to point his finger at me, Cecelia interrupts him.

'I'm perfectly fine with having the food you had yesterday, Mr Ranade. I don't mind real Indian cuisine. In fact, I'd love to taste some.'

Dad starts to shake his head. 'This is too spicy and oily for your taste.'

I want to tell him that if she wishes to act sweet, then why encourage her to act homely? Let her adjust; that's what she intends to do anyway. But I know better than to say anything.

'Mr Ranade, I'll be fine. I love spicy food.' She smiles a bit too broadly and sits on the edge of the table like she owns the place. I picture her munching on our hot, oily *sabji*. I imagine her eyes watering and hands reaching for water after every bite. Her delicate organs would burn down with one bite of our food, if she dared to try it.

'Are you sure you can handle this?' Dad hesitates, looking at me. Apparently, he means to ask if she can handle his daughter rather than the food. I wriggle my brows at him and he shoots me a you-better-behave look. I smile, fill the casserole dish with *rotis* and slide it into the oven.

'*Haan-ji*. I'm sure,' she says. The Indian word sounds funny on her tongue.

My dad murmurs something before disappearing out the door. Having taken half a day off, he can't afford to wait around any longer. He'd be back by nine at night.

When I hear the main door shut and an awkward silence spreads around the house, reality hits me like a tsunami. I'm alone with Cecelia Barnes for the rest of the day. And today is just the first day of the month.

Chapter Three

From the corner of my eye, I see Cecelia pull out a dining chair. Would this woman breathe down my neck as I worked now? I grow uncomfortable when people watch me while I work. It gets distracting. But how would I explain this to her?

I busy my hands in turning the smooth dials on the microwave. Temperature at max, it dings when I set it up for the next five minutes.

'You were thinking of someone special back then, weren't you?'

The question catches me off guard. 'Sorry?'

'You were thinking... of someone special... back then, weren't you?' she repeats, slower this time. I feel indignant.

'I heard you the first time,' I mumble and shift my weight to one foot. I make sure I appear confident before I ask her, 'When?'

'You know when,' she smiles. Her chin is resting on her palm and there is a glint in her eyes. I narrow my eyes, clearly not interested in discussing it.

'I'm sorry.' Her smile dies on her face, probably on seeing my expression. 'I'm not trying to be inquisitive. I am just curious. If you don't want to talk about it, that's fine.'

I resume my work without a word, not knowing what

to say. I did not want to say anything. She doesn't ask any more questions and I'm glad. Plates and glasses clink as I pull them out of the wooden cupboard. She starts to get to her feet, but I gesture for her to sit back down. I'm stuck with this work every afternoon and I'm used to it.

'That's okay.' She stands anyway and helps by arranging knives and forks on the table beside our plates. I guess she does it more out of routine than wanting to be useful. Either way, it is unnecessary.

I unfasten the lid of the cooker and a gust of hot steam blows into our faces. The aroma is mouth-watering. At least to me.

I serve *dal* and hot *rotis* out of the microwave. Out of my peripheral vision, I see Cecelia trying to strike up some conversation, probably to ask a few more useless questions. But each time she opens her mouth, I suddenly become more interested in doing other stuff. Like serving food, checking my phone or watching the pigeon doze off in an empty plant pot outside our kitchen window.

When I finally take a seat next to her, I glance up. But for the first time, her attention is not on me. She is engrossed in frowning at the food in her plate; the fork and knife in her hands.

'We don't generally use a knife and fork to tear a *roti*,' I say.

Hearing my voice, she looks up. 'Then how do you break it?'

'Well, we have hands, you know,' I provide, crossing my arms on the table.

She sets her cutlery aside and pulls her sleeves up,

waiting for me. Is it so difficult to eat with your hands that you'd need instructions?

I tear a piece of *roti* with my fingers, scoop the *sabji* into it and wait for her. She starts to dive in with both her hands.

I stop her midway. 'Don't use both.'

After a couple of attempts, she has a rather long piece of chewy *roti* in her hand.

'Now you dip that either into the *sabji* or *dal*,' I tell her. She dabs the piece in the *sabji*. 'That's it,' I shrug. One thing I like about her is her genuine resolve to learn. She doesn't seem to be mocking our culture.

Her face lights up. She holds her piece of *roti* near my hand, bumping it with the one in mine, and says, 'Cheers.' She asks if she is supposed to eat the blend of rice and *dal* (which I mixed for her) with her hands too. I tell her she could use a spoon or her hands.

She picks up the spoon lying beside her plate and digs into the mountain of rice. 'Mmm… this is good.' With two chews, her jaw slows down and she reaches for her glass of water. 'And spicy!'

I snort, feeling like I'm around a child.

* * *

After we are done, she gets to her feet and walks over to wash her hands, leaving her dirty plate right where it is on the table. I frown. I expected her to be a bit more sensitive, given our little bonding session. She could at least carry her plate to the sink. She'll be staying here for a month and she is already acting like a queen. Who am I? Her servant?

But I don't say anything. If this continues, I always have Dad to complain to. I pick up her plate and drop it into the sink. I wash my hands and start to throw away the remains.

As I take out three ice cream bowls—one for me, one for the queen and the last for my dog—I see Cecelia enter the kitchen again. Without saying a word, she trots towards the sink and turns the tap on. She begins washing plates and bowls with tap water.

'Hey, what are you doing?' I ask, alarmed.

She glances at me as if nothing is wrong. 'Doing the dishes.'

'But why? You don't need to do that.'

'Oh come on.' She waves her hand at me, sending drops of water flying. One lands on my cheek. 'It's nothing. I'm just helping.'

'No, really. Stop. You don't need to do that.' I wipe off the water on my cheek with the back of my hand and walk over to her. 'We have a house maid who does that. Neither my dad nor I do it.' I reach over and close the running tap.

'Maid,' she repeats, putting the plates down. 'You have a regular maid come over to do it.'

'Not just this, she does a lot of other work too—washing clothes, dusting furniture, etc., except cooking, that is.'

'Your maid also does the laundry for you?' she asks, now genuinely interested. 'And cleans up your mess... every day?'

'Uh huh.'

'When does she do all that?'

'Whenever she's free. Ours is not the only house she

works in, so we have handed her our house keys. She comes between 11:00 a.m. and 5:00 p.m., does her work and leaves.'

Cecelia's brown eyes go wide. They look pretty up close. 'She has keys to this house and is free to enter at will?'

'We trust her,' I say shortly and hold a bowl in front of her. 'Ice cream?' She takes it from my hand and starts to lick the ice cream spoon, lost in thought.

After we are done, she asks if she can lie down for a while in the guest room. I'm more than pleased. As soon as I'm sure she is asleep, I rush to my room, lock the door and call Darshak.

Chapter Four

'Hello?' Darshak picks up my call on the fifth ring. His voice sounds distant and thinner than usual; it does so when he warms up after lunch for his regular five-hour rehearsal. Butterfly wings flutter in the pit of my stomach. I hate what his voice does to me even after two years of togetherness.

'Hey, hon,' I say.

I hear, 'Ooooh', and, 'Hey *hon*', 'We miss you, *hon*', in the background. A roar of laughter follows the comments and I realize I'm on speaker.

'Shut up guys!' Darshak says to his band members and then into the phone, 'Gimme two minutes.'

I hear his shoes tap against the floor and a click. The voices subside and eventually die. Darshak must have entered the quiet passageway and closed the door of the soundproof music room behind him. In that silence, I hear the sound of his heavy breathing. Vocal warm ups can get exhausting.

'Sorry about that,' he wheezes. 'So how was your day with the new guest?'

'Eventful,' I say between my teeth. 'Don't ask.'

'She's from America, right? Or was it Canada?'

'Canada,' I mutter, not very keen on discussing her further.

'Wow. And how is she?'

'Fine.'

'No I mean… how does she look?'

I inhale sharply. 'Go to hell, Darshak. I call you after so long and the first thing you want to know is how the new guest is?' I snap. 'She ain't the prime minister of Canada that we need to talk about her, first thing in our convo.'

'Woah! Calm down,' he says, a smile starting to form in his voice. 'Think it was a rough meet.'

'You think?'

'Hey, I didn't mean... I'm sorry I was just asking.'

'I know you were. I just…' I sigh, hauling the Dell onto my lap. I press down the power button on my laptop, hold it for a while, and watch it flicker to life.

It isn't his fault that I am stuck. He is just being a good boyfriend, asking me about my day and all that. I decide to go easy on him. 'Cecelia's good. I mean, not like the other typical aunts and maybe a bit innocent too. She doesn't talk crooked like most elders do. Doesn't ask for my results. And, well, she doesn't look anything like a forty plus woman.'

'Okay… that doesn't sound bad. What's the problem, then?'

I pinch the bridge of my nose while I wait for my laptop to start up. 'The problem is that she is going to stay here for a month. And only I am going to cater to her needs.'

'Why? Your dad…'

'He's busy working all day, so it's just the two of us.'

'Hmm,' he drawls. 'Is that bad?' He fails to understand

what's bad about the situation. Guys always miss what is in between the lines.

'No,' I say. I Google, 'how to survive house guests'. Opening another tab on the side, I type 'Facebook' into it and press enter. 'It's not all that bad… apart from the little downer that I won't be able to attend your rehearsals every day after college, since she'll be alone at home.

'I might have to drop out of our hangouts if Cecelia and I have some other plans. And I'm ditching our trek this month. I also can't talk to you all that much in her presence. So you can't call me whenever you want. You'll have to wait for me to call you.'

Darshak is a part of our college band, which performs every year at our annual function. They also perform at some events outside college that pay, like birthday parties, clubs or receptions. Even though I am not exactly a part of the band, I'm a part of the team. I handle the sound system and mostly all the technical or side stuff, talking to organizers or making sure they don't run into problems last minute. So I'm supposed to attend all their rehearsals, whether I'm of any creative help or not—mostly, I'm not.

Apart from that, all of us are trekkers and plan one trek every three to four months, as a rejuvenating routine. The next one is three weeks from now.

There is a long silence on the other end.

'Hello?' I say into the phone.

More silence.

'Darshak? You there?'

'I can't call you when I want to? You're ditching our pre-planned trek?' He repeats my words in a monotone.

'I won't say no. But like I said, Aunt Cecelia comes first.' I pause to let the news sink in. 'If she's home, then I need to be there too. What with those couriers, delivery men and salesmen knocking at our door at random hours. I can't leave her alone. Or if Dad wants me to spend a particular day with her, show her around the city and all, then I'll have to see that she enjoys it.'

'Who the hell is she? Queen Elizabeth?'

I smile. Now that we share the same frustration, I feel better. 'She doesn't know anyone else from Mumbai. As a matter of fact, she doesn't know anyone else in all of India.'

'Then why come to a country you don't know anything about?' he snaps. 'What is she doing now?'

'Sleeping, I suppose.'

'We'll see how we can get around this. We'll sneak you out quietly if we have to.'

'Don't be silly…' I start.

'That we'll see. Let's not talk about it and ruin this time.' We let it rest for a while and, to my great relief, change the topic. I scroll through the news feeds and 'like' a few posts and profile pictures. 'How's Rocky, by the way?'

My mind goes blank and I imagine the face of the desperate, lonely dog. 'Oh no!' I push my laptop on the bed and spring up.

'What?' Darshak asks alarmed.

'Nothing. He's tied up, because Cecelia is scared of dogs. I forgot to unleash him.' I dash out to our balcony, which is attached to the living room, and slide the door open. A small wooden dog house, which I built when I was in fifth standard to welcome a tiny pup eight years ago, sits in a corner.

The little house is painted bright pink—the paint now peeling off—with multi-coloured flowers doodled on the rooftop. It is much too feminine and kiddish for a full grown, vicious-looking canine like Rocky.

But I was a wide-eyed, pony-tailed kid in love with frilly frocks and stuffed toys. The dog house was one of my best works of art at the time. And Rocky loved it. Period.

White linen covered in drawings of puppy faces and an empty bowl lie inside the dog house. Basil, money plants, hibiscus and my mother's favourite white roses sway on the other end of the balcony, far enough where Rocky's chain wouldn't reach.

I hear the clinks of the chain and before I have a chance to look, it tangles around my left leg. A fuzzy coat of fur jumps to hug my waist.

'I'm so sorry, baby!' I balance the phone between my ear and shoulder and bend down to snap Rocky's leash open. I grab his quivering body and kiss his head.

'Go bite Cecelia Aunty,' I mutter. His bushy tail beats against my back while I rummage inside his dog house to find his chicken bone. 'She's the reason you're tied here in the first place.'

When I push the bone into Rocky's mouth, he spins around twice, wags his tail and follows me to my room.

'Sorry,' I say into the phone. 'You still there?'

'You know, sometimes I curse my fate and ask God why I wasn't born a dog. Life would be so much better.'

I run my hand over Rocky's smooth fur and rest it just

below his neck. A slow rumble vibrates in his throat and I laugh. 'I'm not interested in your bone, Rocksy. Once you finish this, I'm gonna eat you anyway.' I bury my face in his fur and plant a forceful kiss on the top of his forehead. Thumping his tail twice, he kicks to his feet and strides past me to sit in another corner of the room.

'Heartbreaker.' I sigh. 'Hello?' I return to Darshak on the line now that I've been abandoned.

'Yeah, I'm here. Just listening to my girlfriend flirt with someone else,' I hear him snort. 'You talk to the dog as if he is your lover or something.'

'Hey, don't call him a dog,' I scowl. 'And why, he is my lover. The first love of my life.'

'Yeah, right. And I'm the sidekick.'

I hear the click of a door opening on the other end of the line. 'Break time's up, Romeo. We're starting up,' Purti says.

'Coming.' Darshak enters into the noise of instruments all playing at the same time and voices chattering away.

'I wish I was there,' I mutter, hearing the chaos and imagining my presence amongst the others.

'I know,' he says.

'Practise well. Rock that stage at our annual function,' I say.

'That we will. But only if you're there.'

'Of course, I will be there. What made you think I'd miss the big show?'

'Enough, you guys.' I hear Purti's voice again. 'Even I don't talk to my boyfriend so much.'

'That's because he hardly calls you.' That must be Hiten with his smart mouth waiting to go off at the slightest hint.

'That's because he is busy and not jobless like other people in this room, right now,' Purti says and they launch into a verbal war.

'Neha…' Darshak starts.

'I know,' I sigh, trying to let my smile linger in my voice, which isn't difficult hearing the two wild cats hurl words at each other in the background. 'Time to hang up.'

Every time I have to disconnect Darshak's call, something inside me sinks. It isn't an overwhelming feeling, just a hint of disappointment. The way you feel when you see a waiter carry yummy food, but it turns out it isn't for you. Had I gone to college today, I'd be with him and my gang in that room watching them go over their music.

If only.

Before hanging up he puts the phone on speaker, so I can speak with everyone.

'We're having loads of fun, now that you're not here.'

'See you on Monday.' A pause. 'Or not.'

'Go to hell, y'all,' I pipe up amidst their laughter.

'I'll meet you in the evening,' Purti says after the laughter dies down. She and I make a gross smooching sound over the telephone and I hear a few disgusted grunts.

'Sometimes, I believe everybody else is in a relationship with you except me,' Darshak says and I chuckle.

When I disconnect to the sound of distant laughter, I glance around the room. Rocky gnaws his bone slowly, his eyelids drooping with held back sleep. It seems like I've returned from an out-of-body experience. For those few minutes, I was in that music den with everyone and not in my room, alone, gliding through pointers on how to survive houseguests.

Chapter Five

In the evening, I throw on a green, full-sleeved top and black dhoti pants before hopping down the lane to meet Purti at our regular hangout. Her Scooty is parked outside CCD. I peep into the café through its glass door and find her sleeping in a corner, her head resting on the wall behind her and her mouth open. I sink into a chair beside her and poke her stomach.

'What the…' her eyes fly open. She strokes the spot and growls when she sees me, then drops her head on the opposite arm rest. 'Gimme five minutes.'

I poke her again, making her twitch.

'Stop!' she says, without raising her head. Purti is the female lead singer of Darshak's band and my best friend. She is an all-rounder, both shape and talent wise. Her extra-large dresses cling to her hefty body for dear life and she isn't blessed with the prettiest face in town. But personally, I'd give up everything I have if I could get a voice and fingers like hers in return.

She hits every note with precision and enriches the background music with her keyboard. You only have to listen to her once and you're sure to lay your heart at her feet. I always make sure she takes good care of her voice—gargling with lukewarm water, not drinking anything too cold, not eating too much roadside food and always drinking enough water. Like now.

I fish out the water bottle from her bag to check if she has been drinking enough. It's empty. Satisfied, I drop it back and with nothing better to do, I pull out her phone. I unlock the screen with her 'S' unlock pattern. How cliché to make your darling's initial your pattern. Not cliché, lame.

I open her WhatsApp and scroll through Suraj's chat. She had asked him if he was free a few days ago. He hadn't replied and so after a few minutes, she'd sent, 'Suraj! At least don't ignore me.'

Then he had said he was having a, 'Cuppa with his buddies.' And yes, he was free.

'So let's watch the movie *Take It Easy*. I wanna watch it with you,' Purti had texted.

'Okay,' he had replied.

And the conversation seemed to have ended there. The next afternoon, Purti had asked him where he was and if it was possible for him to come for an afternoon show. He had said that he was in college and that he would let her know.

He never got back to her; at least not through text, because their chats pretty much end there. Purti seemed to have called him.

'Called you. I'm at the theatre. Call me ASAP,' she'd texted. There is one reply from him four hours later. I frown into her phone, feeling a little angry at the response.

'Sorry sweets. I fell asleep,' I read aloud. Purti wakes up with a start and snatches her phone so quickly from my hand that I stare at her. 'What was that?' I ask.

She manages to exit the chat window and lock her phone before dropping it into her bag. Then, she changes her mind and puts it back on the table. 'He might call,' she mutters, laying her head against the cushion and going right back to sleep.

'What is this, Pop? I'm here to meet you and all you do is sleep.' I pretend to get up and walk away. 'I'm leaving.' She doesn't budge, and I sigh, my hand on my hip. 'Purti, enough, okay? This is annoying.'

She can tell when my anger is real and when I'm faking it. She lifts her head, runs her fingers over her face, pressing them momentarily against her eyes, and peeks at me through her fingers.

'He ditched you again,' I say. I don't name names. I don't have to. 'And you let him get away with it.'

Purti suddenly develops an interest in the menu stuck under the glass table top. 'No. I'm going with regular cappuccino. What will you have?'

'Lemonade,' I say and plunge back into the topic. 'You forgave him.' It isn't a question. Knowing Purti and how much she loves Suraj, she must have called him in the evening to ask if he was fine. And that it was not a problem at all that he failed to show up. After all, college can be tiring. Like sitting on the last bench in an air-conditioned classroom involved building a five-year financial plan.

'He called me,' she says, taking a sip of water from her glass. 'And apologized.'

'Stop covering up for him. He's nothing but a bad boyfriend.'

There is hardly anyone in the café, apart from a couple sitting and talking quietly in one corner, their coffees untouched in front of them. A server is at our table. 'Your orders, Ma'am.'

'Cappuccino and kiwi lemonade.' I stare at a picture of a cheese toast on the wall. 'And one chilli cheese toastizza.'

'Anything else?'

I shake my head.

'It's hard not to love a bad boy who is just a good boy hiding behind a mask, you know,' Purti says and I turn to her. She rests her head back, gazing idly at the ceiling.

'He is *not* a good boy,' I point out to her. 'And how many months will you spend hoping he treats you well one of these days?'

She closes her eyes. 'Don't forget how he stands by me every time someone threatens to hurt me.'

'So?' I inch forward, now sitting on the edge of my seat, my knee almost touching hers. 'Even I do that. And Shirish and Darshak. And I'm sure you'd do the same if it came to him. But that's not enough!'

'Will you just stop?' Purti turns in my direction, her eyes red, from lack of sleep or anger, I don't know. 'Can't you just see me happy for once?'

The couple sitting across turns to look at us. I lean back in my chair, just enough to let Purti know I am taken aback by her comment. But I hold my peace, not wanting to ruin this mood and attract unwanted attention. Instead, I watch as the waiter trots back towards us, balancing our order on his tray. He lays our drinks in front of us on the table. I snatch mine up and take a swig. My throat, chest, then stomach shudder as the chilled drink travels down.

'I'm sorry,' Purti says. I can feel her studying me through

her dark lashes enhanced by winged liner. It makes her eyes look alive. She only wears it occasionally, though—whenever she has to go meet her guy.

'I love him and he says he loves me too.' She wraps her fingers around the hot coffee mug and picks it up. 'And I know he does because when we meet, it's like he can't keep his eyes or hands off me.' The corner of her lip lifts up. 'We're inseparable. Really.'

I twirl the ice in my glass and hear it clink against the sides. 'How was practice today?' I'm not going to say anything more on the topic, and not because I'm hurt by her previous remark.

Well, maybe, I am. A little. The last thing I want is to see Purti cry over some guy and regret not warning her about him. But if she is *this* happy to be with someone I don't approve of, I will accept it and support her; even if it's a married man, twice her age who would swear never to break her.

No, that'd be too much. I'd lock her up till she got over him.

But Suraj is fine. If you look at the bright side, he is quite a respectable guy. He never seems to demean Purti. And he seems genuinely proud of her talent. So he just might be a good guy underneath after all.

Okay, now that's an exaggeration.

'And his parents are coming. So he can't come for the trek,' Purti's saying. I catch her last words just in time to summon a shocked expression.

'What? Not coming for the trek?' I don't ask her who, in case I make it obvious I haven't been paying attention.

'Yeah. So that drops the number by four.' Purti sinks her teeth into a piece of crisp bread with melted cheese on it. 'Now, if anybody else cancels I swear I'll kick him in the gut.'

I laugh, not because I find it amusing, but because I'm genuinely scared. If four people have dropped out already, the fun we are supposed to have has been halved. And I haven't told anyone I'm not coming either.

'Really. It just ruined my mood today,' Purti sighs. 'Anyway, you're coming, right?'

I gulp my drink and laugh nervously. That is the most fake laugh of my life. 'Of course. What made you think otherwise?' But it satisfies her and she drops the topic.

My phone vibrates in my back pocket. I reach for it: *Home calling*.

'Who's it?' Purti pokes her armrest with an elbow and peeks at my phone, her hair covering the sides of her face. Her eyes trail up to meet mine. 'I thought there was no one in your house all day.'

I frown. 'There isn't, but remember I told you about a Canadian aunt coming to stay with us?'

I watch Purti blink once before her eyes glint. 'Oh yeah! But why would she call you?'

I shrug and swipe right. 'Hello.'

'Nay-ha, where are you?' The accented voice sounds panicky. My back straightens.

'Just around the corner. Is everything all right?'

'No. Nothing is all right…' she says and holds the mouthpiece away from her. 'Will you please wait? *Ruko, ruko!*'

I spring to my feet, gesture to Purti to give me a second and rush out of the café for better network.

'*Arey, ye roj ka kaam hai*!' someone yells saying it's an everyday chore.

'What's happening?' I ask to no avail. The argument fires up a notch and I can hardly catch a few words.

'No.'

'Yes.'

'You'll ruin it!'

'Haan. Room *bhi*.'

I hear distant barks on the other end. Rocky. I imagine him cowering in a corner, fighting to shut these voices out and my thoughts screech to a sudden halt.

'What the hell is going on?' I march inside the cafe and start to collect my handbag. I wave off Purti's attempts to ask me questions, since I don't know anything myself.

Purti touches her mug to her lips and gulps down her coffee in one swig. She grabs two half-eaten toasts, slaps a note of five hundred on the counter on our way out and taps her foot while the girl counts change.

'Quick!' I say. Purti snatches the money, leaving the girl with a hefty tip that we'll collect tomorrow, and we dash out the door.

'I don't know what's happening, but this woman is ruining everything. I knew it was a bad idea to hand over the keys to her,' Cecelia says.

'Is the maid home?' I ask tentatively. The muffled voice of a woman behind Cecelia sounds barbaric and loud. Nobody else I know speaks that way other than Sangeeta Mausi.

'Yeah, she is.'

'Okay, hold on. Don't do anything till I come home. Can I speak to her?'

'Yes,' she says.

A shift of hands on the other end creates a disturbance on the line. When Sangeeta Mausi speaks, she sounds pissed off and equally unable to control her anger.

'Ye kaun hai gori aurat? Mera roj ka kaam aap jante ho, baby. *Wo kuch karne nahi deti.'* (Who is this white woman? You know my daily duties, child. She won't let me do anything.)

Purti starts her Scooty, tossing a weary look behind her. I purse my lips and try to calm the situation. 'Don't do anything yet. I'll come and see what the matter is. Please hold on for five minutes.'

A minute later, as Purti drives around trying to find the right place to park, I sprint up the stairs on the second floor and ring the doorbell twice. The door flies open and I see Cecelia's expression. It looks like she has guzzled a bottle of cough syrup. Sangeeta Mausi's nostrils are flaring behind her, a long, smooth piece of wood in her hand.

I close the door behind me and look around to hunt for Rocky. He is tied up in the balcony, his head poking out from behind the curtain and his tongue hanging out, dripping with saliva. He huffs for breath as the leash squeezes his neck like a snake and twists around his leg. I wince at the sight.

I rush to loosen the grip of his collar, pet him, scratch under his neck and pacify him to some extent. I pull myself out of the death grip of his paws and stand in the kitchen. Cecelia sits on a chair adjacent to me. Mausi leans against the kitchen sink.

Cecelia narrows her eyes at Mausi, who shoots annoyed looks at her in return and I listen to how the quarrel began. And by the end of it, I fight to maintain an indifferent expression. My face twitches madly and I want to break into stomach-aching, eye-watering laughter.

The story is that shortly after I left in the late afternoon to catch up with my friends from my building and Purti, Cecelia awoke and freshened up. With nothing better to do, she decided it would be wise to help us around the house and relieve me of some of the burden. So she trotted towards the washing machine and peered at the instruction sticker plastered on it.

When she had read it and started to dump all the clothes into the machine, a click and twist of the main door had made her jump. Since it wasn't time for my dad or me to return, she had rushed out with a sharp kitchen knife to defend herself, if need be. Sangeeta Mausi had dumped her bag on the shoe rack and had turned around to see an unknown woman flashing a blade at her.

Both women had stared at each other for a second before Cecelia had croaked, 'Are you the maid?'

Sangeeta Mausi had eyed the knife and nodded in fear, not knowing exactly what she was agreeing to.

'And you have the house keys?' Cecelia had examined her from head to toe.

Mausi had had no clue what Cecelia said, so she had made a hand gesture to indicate sweeping the floor. Somehow they had managed to communicate and Cecelia had dropped her shoulders in relief.

After half an hour of watching like a hawk while Mausi

dusted and swept, Cecelia had wandered into her room to read a book knowing the woman knew how to do her job. But after about fifteen minutes, she had heard loud pounding noises, like someone whipping the marble floor. She had sprinted out to see what the source of the sound was and had almost flipped out when she saw what Mausi had been doing.

She had been beating up the clothes on our common bathroom floor with a thick, smooth handheld piece of wood and a soap bar by her side. Mausi had apparently fished out all the clothes from the washing machine and had now been thrashing them so they were clean.

Cecelia had seized her shoulder, hauled her up and scolded her for ruining our clothes. Sangeeta Mausi, offended by this rudeness and by having someone question her expert work ethics for the first time, had started fighting back.

And when both of them could only bark at each other for some time, making exaggerated hand gestures, but failing to understand a word of what the other was saying, Cecelia had dialled my number and had summoned me to the scene.

'That is how Mausi is used to washing our clothes, Aunty,' I say at the end of Cecelia's narration with occasional interruptions. Sangeeta Mausi had feared that Cecelia would say something against her, so she had butted in every now and then to explain her side of the story.

Not that it matters. The issue is too trivial.

'I can't have her washing my clothes,' Cecelia says. She rises to her feet and heads to the bathroom, 'I'll do this on my own.'

'Ye sab kya hai, baby?' (What's going on, child?) Mausi's tone softens as she directs her question at me. I raise my head to meet her gaze. I notice her drooping eyes, the wrinkled skin around them and her sagging frame. She wears a beige coloured, hand-me-down saree and a jasmine festoon attached to the back of her head. She smells of jasmine too.

She is a fierce woman if provoked, but a very soft-spoken, loving lady if respected.

'Sorry, Mausi. She is not used to our way of working,' I say in Hindi and fill up two glasses of cold water, handing her one. *'Agli baar, sirf humare kapde dhona.'* (Next time, only wash our clothes.)

'Roj wohi karti hu,' (that's what I do every day) she says, drinking the water, rinsing her glass and placing it back on the shelf. 'Thank you.' She runs her hand over my head and gives me a kind smile before striding past.

I watch Cecelia fish out her bundle of clothes sprawled across the bathroom floor, wrinkle her nose in disgust at the mess and make the same face at Mausi before marching off to the washing machine. Mausi jerks her chin up while shooting Cecelia similar scornful looks. She pulls her saree up to her knees and bends over the mountain of clothes. My heart constricts with withdrawn sympathy for both of them.

Cecelia runs her fingers over the sticker on the machine, reading the guidelines as she does. I'd have asked to help her with the instructions, but I conclude that she'll figure it out. And anyway, I need a nap before I explode from facing another fight.

Chapter Six

That night, Dad is accompanied by Bob Uncle and Geeta Aunty when he comes home. They are his colleagues and they had accompanied him to the airport to receive Cecelia that morning.

Dad brings in two bottles of Sula Wine, four cans of beer, a Coke and some bags of snacks and dumps them on the dining table. He asks me to sort them all out and set plates. They are going to throw a private welcome party for Cecelia, partly because it is a Saturday night and partly to make her comfortable. Cecelia is touched by this gesture.

'Nanu, I have a surprise for you,' Dad says to me when I balance my drink in one hand and a plate full of chicken wings and boiled salted chickpeas in the other. I place the plate in front of Bob Uncle who pops a wing into his mouth. I sit next to Dad.

'What surprise?' I sip my favourite homemade Coke float, a scoop of vanilla ice cream floating in the Coke. It tastes heavenly.

Dad pulls out an envelope from his shirt pocket.

'What's this?' I place my glass down and turn to him. I narrow my eyes at the envelope, turn it over and hold it against the light to scan it before tearing it open. I am hoping for cash.

'Tickets,' he says and beams, looking utterly pleased with himself.

'To?'

'Just open it and see for yourself.'

I kick out my feet and cross them in a lotus posture. Though curious, I am a tad bit cautious about expecting too much. I've been getting a lot of surprises from Dad in the past few days, none of which are pleasant.

I tear the envelope open and two tickets fall into my lap. I read the words at the top.

'We're going to…' I stare at the words for a long time, trying to bring myself to believe them. They're tickets to Adlabs Imagica (AI), the Disneyland of India. Excitement starts to swell inside me.

He pats my knee. 'Adlabs Imagica! Yes!'

'Are you serious?'

'Of course. Everything's been arranged,' he says, taking a long slurp from his drink and letting the words sink in. 'You'll be staying at a nice hotel near the park and spending two full days there.'

It takes me a while to grasp the news. Once I do, I almost fall off my seat in delight. 'Oh my god!' I leap up from the sofa and lunge at him, hugging him so tight he is nearly out of breath. 'I love you so much! You're better than I thought.'

'You're welcome.' When I release him, he pulls away from me and gasps for air. 'But just remember your dad is getting old. So think before expressing your love openly like that.'

Laughter erupts in the room and Geeta Aunty plucks the

tickets from my hand to have a closer look. 'Looks like fun.' She scans the papers and nods toward Bob Uncle.

'Thank you so much!' I grin at Dad, unable to stop smiling for some reason. 'How did you know I wanted to go there?'

He shrugs. 'Caught you surfing the internet last week. I think you were checking out the price of tickets.' Yeah, I had been. And I had tons of videos and images of rides saved on my laptop.

'Lucky lass. You've got a great dad.' Geeta Aunty tosses the tickets on the table and smiles at me.

I stare at Dad as if he's just sprouted angel wings and a halo above his head. 'And a great mum. All in one,' I add. We share a silent, loving look before I break into another big grin. 'Imagica. I can't believe this!' I am feeling as enthused as a nine-year-old, but I don't really care.

My friends will go crazy if they find out. I'll be the first person amongst us to visit AI. We're bored of holidaying at Essel World and Water Kingdom. AI is a new theme park that was recently inaugurated, the only park that we haven't explored. And we have been discussing going there for quite some time now.

'When are we going?' I have forgiven Dad for bringing Cecelia home and shoving her at me.

'Not we. You and Cecelia are going. The trip is about a week and a half from now. Look at that date on the tickets, no?' Dad examines a ticket to hunt for the dates. 'Here.' He turns them towards me, pointing at it, so I can have a closer look.

But I'm already frozen in place. And I do not do a very

good job of hiding my horror. 'Aunty Cecelia and I?' I hiss. The bubble of excitement and anticipation forming in my heart bursts.

'Yes. I'd have loved to accompany you, but it's a weekday and I have an important dinner meeting. We've been suffering a liability on our project and I can't afford to take leave. I have already talked to Cecelia about this and she is pretty excited.'

Cecelia sips her wine in silence, refusing to make eye contact with either of us when I glare at her. I noted how she smiled when Dad pressed the envelope into my hand, how she chuckled with the others when I had literally jumped on him with joy. But now she merely looks gloomy and impassive. This is as opposed to Bob Uncle and Geeta Aunty who are rather jolly about the whole thing. I think Cecelia picked up on my negative vibes.

Good, I think. I do not care about veiling them either.

That night I do not chat much, neither does Cecelia. She talks with the others, laughs with them, but when our eyes meet, her smile fades. She tries to initiate it, but I avoid eye contact.

After a while, even she gives up.

Chapter Seven

'Dad what's for breakfaaa—' I yawn as I enter the kitchen the next morning and stop in my tracks.

Cecelia peers over her shoulder. 'Hey,' she says and resumes doing whatever she is doing. 'Morning.'

'Umm...' What the hell are you doing here? Who gave you the permission to enter our kitchen? You are a freaking guest, so act like one! I bite back all the venom starting to form on the tip of my tongue. Instead I ask her, 'Where's Dad?'

'Mr Ranade has gone out to buy lilies for breakfast.'

I choke on the water I had pulled out from the refrigerator. 'What is he bringing us?'

'Lilies. Or...' she pulls her brows together, trying to remember something. 'Lilies. That's what it sounded like. I was confused too, but then I thought they must be named after those flowers. It's a south Indian speciality he said.'

I slap my head, making sure she doesn't see me when I do. 'They're called *idlies*. Not lilies.' I hide a grin. 'Made out of *udid*.'

I know she has no clue what I'm talking about, but she nods anyway. Her effort to stay out of my way and in my good books is so obvious, it's funny and also intriguing. I have no plans to make it any easier for her.

'What are you doing?' I watch while she plucks three plates and silverware, placing them on the table.

'Just fixing the table, so we can serve ourselves as soon as the food comes.' She starts to wipe the dishes with the clean cloth I had used last night. The corners of my mouth turn down and I nod. For one thing, she's doing my share of the chores without realizing it. So I let her continue and stroll out to read the morning newspapers.

Cecelia turns up in the living room some time later balancing two coffee mugs in her hands. She offers one to me.

'Thanks.' I smile and move to one side of the sofa to make room for her.

'You're welcome.' She drops down next to me and pokes her head into the newspaper in my hand. I sip my coffee and read the same headline thrice. Her warm breath on my shoulder and the strong fragrance of her perfume annoys the heck out of me.

I exhale, fold the paper in half and twist in my seat to face her. 'You wanna read first?' She blinks at me, then shakes her head. 'Then mind giving me a little space, maybe?' Okay. That was rude, I know, but is there any other way to get her off my back?

'Oh, of course. I'm sorry. Didn't mean to intrude.' She pulls her lips into a forced smile. 'Actually, I got you something from Canada. I'd have given it to you last night, but I didn't get a chance.'

She means, 'You're such a brat, you didn't give me a chance.' But she is polite.

I toss the paper onto the side table and ask her,

genuinely interested. 'What is it?'

She smiles genuinely this time. 'Let me bring it.' She sets the mug down and rushes to the guest room. She comes back with a bag full of… well, just full. It is tough to guess what could be inside. She unzips it. 'I did not know what you would like, so I got a little of everything.'

I take the bag from her and squint as I look inside it. It is filled with fancily wrapped gifts. 'All this, for me?' I ask her, a little amazed at her generosity. She nods.

I fish out a flat, soft present wrapped in golden paper with a silver ribbon across it. I suppose it's a book. I'm right. On unwrapping it, a brand new paperback copy of *Nights in Rodanthe* by Nicholas Sparks falls out.

I turn a page and suddenly, the book weighs a hundred pounds more in my hands. Slanted writing in blue ink and a personal message adorns the first page. I run my fingers over it.

It is a signed copy. There is a freaking autograph of Nicholas Sparks in the copy!

I read out the scribbled personalized message. 'To the lovely, Nayha. Happy reading. Nicholas Sparks.' I stare open mouthed at the book for a while and then up at Cecelia.

'When did he…?' I'm too stunned to finish my question.

'I met him during one of his meet and greets. I think he misspelled your name, but I didn't know the spelling either. So he wrote what he thought fit.'

'Are you kidding me?' I blink back at the book. 'I'd pay to read his shopping list. He can misspell my name any damn way he wants.' I drop the book in my lap and stretch my arms around her for a hug. 'Thanks a lot, Aunty! It means a lot to me.'

A bashful smile spreads across her face. 'It's nothing.' When we pull away, she wrinkles her nose. 'And please call me Cecelia. Drop the "Aunty".'

I think it over for a second. She doesn't look like an aunt. At nearly forty-two years of age, she looks like a woman in her early thirties. But since she has spoiled me with such an incredible gift, I'll try to do this one thing for her.

'Okay, Cecelia.' It feels odd, at first, to call her by her name, but I decide I'll get used to it. 'Thank you.'

I unpack the next present, which is bulkier and covered in wrapping paper with tiny red hearts all over it. It is Taylor Swift's new studio album, the platinum edition. A few Taylor-themed goodies are crowded inside another bag. They include a set of guitar picks with her stunning face on them, a huge poster featuring her in her adorable black shorts, a mug with some of her song lyrics inscribed on it and a 50 ml perfume, Incredible Things.

I gaze at the bottle for a long time, unable to believe I'm holding it. 'Why am I getting so lucky with gifts lately?' I say, spraying the perfume from the vibrant bottle onto the back of my hand and breathing in the fragrance. It smells mature and something I can imagine the adult Taylor wearing in NY. 'This is a dream. Thank you so much!'

'You like it?'

'Ab-so-lutely!'

The third present is a casual white tank top with a Canadian maple leaf on it and a pair of shorts. Another present is a box of assorted chocolates and the last one is the bag itself. I put my arms around Cecelia's neck again, giving her a gentle, heartfelt hug. I thank her again for bestowing me with such unusual gifts.

'How did you know I liked Taylor Swift?' I ask when I pull away.

'What teenage girl doesn't?'

I smile, stroking the glossy mug with the lyrics of the song *Clean* on it. 'Did you get something for Dad too?'

'Oh yeah, for him and our colleagues. I'll give it to them after our meeting.'

'What is it?' I stuff all the presents back into the bag and start to fold the pretty wrapping paper. 'I swear not to tell anyone.'

'You cross your heart and hope to die?' She wiggles her eyebrows.

I what?

She drops the ribbon into the bag, helping me pack. 'That's like a grown-up pinky promise. We say, "I cross my heart," to assure someone we are speaking the truth, promising not to tell anyone. Do you?'

'Yeah!'

'It's nothing. Just some fancy wine for everyone.'

We work in silence for a few seconds.

'I like your accent,' I mumble when she gets to her feet to collect our coffee mugs. She stops and stares at me, arching a brow. She's probably surprised that I'm aiming praise at her and not a sneer or a sarcastic remark. She smiles.

It is my first attempt at acknowledging her and I

surprise myself when I say it. But then I lower my guard.

Frankly, she isn't a twisted, prodding aunt like I had expected her to be. In fact, she is quite the opposite: kind, gentle and warm-hearted. Maybe I feel this way because she got me all these presents. Or maybe it is my guilt going into overdrive. Whatever it is, the least she deserves is a compliment.

Besides, I do like her accent.

'And I like yours.' She points at me.

'And… why is that?'

She shrugs. 'Because people I like speak in that accent.' I stare at her to gauge any hint of a lie, but she sounds sincere. I hesitate, fearing I might just develop too much of a soft spot for her, but then I return her smile. It's the least I can do.

Chapter Eight

As soon as we finish with our Sunday morning breakfast, I retreat to my room and send pictures of all the presents Cecelia got for me to our WhatsApp group. Girls voice their envy and they ask if I can introduce them to my aunt.

While I type away another boastful reply about how I'll post a picture of my signed copy of *Nights in Rodanthe* everywhere, Shirish pokes fun at me.

'What's with this Sparkling guy?' he says in between dozens of responses that read, 'Wow', and, 'I'm so jealous', and, 'This is awesome'.

'He writes some romance crap. These gals are crazy,' Hiten texts.

And that is the end of the world. We begin to bash him.

'Shut up, Hita! He's the best.'

'What about that football crap that you keep watching? Do you even learn anything from it?'

'Reading books and good ones is definitely better than watching TV all day with your legs curled up and popcorn and chips littered all around you. Oh wait, that would be alcohol and cigarettes, now.'

'He's sparkling amongst the brightest stars in the sky. His name itself says he's a star, get it? Unlike y'all.'

'His books are so moving. You'll never understand the beauty of his writing.'

Frustrated, all the boys quit the group together. Purti, as the admin, does not bother to add them again.

I call Darshak. 'What is wrong with you all?'

'Sorry. I've promised not to be partial to you. I can't say a word.'

'Fine then! Sulk all day.' I disconnect. He calls me twice after about a minute. When I do not pick up the call, my phone buzzes once with a message.

'I'm sorry, Neha. I'll tell you if you promise not to tell anyone,' it reads.

No reply.

'Come ON, princess,' he texts again. He calls me mushy names very rarely, almost never. And I like when he gets all frantic and panicky over me.

'Call,' I reply in one word and pick up his next call on the fourth ring.

'Listen,' he blurts out even before I say a hello. 'We were bored of the endless sparkling talk and the insults showered upon us, so we decided to teach you a lesson. Unless you apologize, we'll stay out of that group.'

I yawn. 'Do you feel the same?'

'No! No. I just had to go with them since, you know, I'm a guy too…'

'Good.' I try not to smile. He is a sweetheart. It is very difficult to stay mad at him for too long.

'So?' he asks.

'So what?'

'Are we on talking terms? I mean, I hope there's no problem between us. We can play-act we're with our respective groups.'

I think over it for a minute. Can I risk going against my gang of girls for my guy? 'Okay.'

'Yes! This is going to be fun.' I hear a grin in his voice that makes me smile. 'So what are you doing this evening?'

I check my nails and decide they need painting. 'Nothing, as of now.'

'Great! So I have tickets to—'

'No tickets!' I cry, springing up on the bed before I realize it. Rocky squirms beside me and I run my hand over his furry back, calming both of us in the process.

'What?'

'Nothing. Sorry, continue.' He doesn't need to know that I'm going to AI with Cecelia yet. I will talk to Dad first and tell him I've other plans with my friends, so I can't go with Cecelia, which otherwise I'd have loved to. Sorry.

I don't want to appear rude, especially after all the gifts that she got for me, but I also don't want to go with her.

'...Will be fun. Should we go?' Darshak's saying.

'Where?' I ask, registering his last few words.

'Are you listening to me, Neha? Where is your freaking attention?'

'I'm sorry. I was just...' I groan, back in the present. 'Nevermind, so you've got tickets to?'

He sighs. 'To an English play at Prithvi Theatre. You'll

love it. It's about how today's generation thinks and our clashes with older people. It's supposed to be hilarious. At 9 o'clock.'

'Hmm.' I want to go with him and have a good laugh at something other than my life. And this looks like a perfect way out of everything. 'I'm in. Who else is coming?'

'No one. Just the two of us.'

I smile. Even more perfect.

Chapter Nine

'Dad!' I kick the door of his study room and barge in. The door closes by itself. He looks at me over his reading glasses. 'Whatchu doin'?' I collapse on the sofa beside his chair and rest my legs on the opposite hand rest. I especially love to sprawl on this sofa, because it is the 'forbidden' sofa. You are not supposed to sprawl on it.

'Put your feet down!'

This is his study and Dad hates it if he is disturbed while he tries to work. But I make sure such trivial rules don't apply to me. 'What is it?' he bookmarks the page he is reading.

I'd thought about exactly how I'd break the news to him—the news that I am going to Prithvi Theatre that night and I can't go to AI with Cecelia, because I am accountable for most of the events in our annual function.

But when he stares at me like I've just killed someone, I stammer. Lying always gets the better of me where lying to my dad is concerned. 'Ah... actually, I...'

'Mr Ranade?' Cecelia knocks on his door, partially pushing it open. 'May I?'

Dad slaps my legs down and nods at her. See? This was what I meant when I said you lose your freedom when you have guests over. I slide to one end of the sofa and make room for her. Cecelia enters, nudging the door to close it behind her. 'Am I interrupting a father-daughter conversation?'

'Oh no, not at all.' He pats the empty spot beside me where only some time ago my legs had been chilling. 'Please.'

'Thank you.'

I roll my eyes at this formality.

'Actually, I wanted to talk about Adlabs Imagica,' she says and my ears prick up. She has my rapt attention.

'What about it?' Dad takes off his glasses, places the book on the nearest table and folds his arms across his chest.

Wow, Daddy, never gave *me* so much attention.

'I don't think I will be able to go. I have some unfinished work to complete.'

Wait. What?

'Work?'

My back is ramrod straight. I struggle to look shocked and sad when she nods. A feeling of hope and excitement starts to expand inside me. Was she, as remote the possibility was, cancelling her plan?

'What work that can't wait?' Dad prods. I shoot him a look that says, don't push her. It is her decision not to come, so we should respect it. After all, it might be some critical, tricky work that needs her attention. But I don't think he notices.

'Well, we have this presentation to make. And I haven't even started yet.'

'Isn't one week enough?'

'No,' she mumbles. I have to lean closer to catch her words. 'It's not.'

'If there's anything I can do to help you with it or even Geeta or Bob, let us know. We wouldn't mind. You know that.'

A thoughtful, only-grown-ups-will-understand glance passes between the two of them. 'No. That's part of my work on the team. I can handle it, but I can't go. Neha should probably get one of her friends to go instead of me.'

I gasp. Was this really happening?

'No,' Dad is quick to add, crushing my hopes. 'She's too young to go there. And moreover, she's going for the first time, so I can't risk that.'

I pout.

'Maybe you could somehow squeeze in the two days?' Dad asks hopefully.

'No, I can't!' Cecelia snaps, holding his gaze. 'I'm sorry.' Startled at her sudden reaction, I raise a brow and decide to keep mum. She hasn't cast a single look my way.

Dad nods. 'Then I think I'll have to cancel it.'

'What?' I look at him, forgetting I'd decided to zip my lips only a second ago. 'Why cancel it? I mean I could go with...' I rack my brain to come up with less scandalous names. Not that it matters. Given a choice, I'd drag Darshak along, no questions asked. But I couldn't possibly say that.

'No friends, Neha. It's very far and I can't send two girls alone there. She'll be as young and naïve as you.' He assumes I'd take one of my girlfriends. He is more naïve than I am.

'I can ask my friends to get tickets,' I add hopefully. 'On

the same day. And then perhaps—'

'I said no.'

That is the end of it.

I wouldn't want to go with anybody else if I can't go with my friends, except my dad. But he is apparently busier than our prime minister.

It crushes me to abandon such a perfect plan. I doubt that everyone in our group could find time on the same day to visit the wonderland, especially during January in the midst of all the prep.

'Pardon me,' Cecelia says, pulling a chain to stop my train of thought. She drums her fingers on the armrest, gives us a tight-lipped smile, apologizes again and excuses herself.

* * *

'Didn't expect this from you,' Dad says, picking his book up, when the door clicks shut. I turn to him.

'What?'

He takes his time putting his glasses back on and turning to the page he was last reading. 'I didn't expect you to be so cold, especially seeing as you're my daughter. We're known to be the best hosts. Your mom was always the best host,' he says, his brows knit so close together they almost touch.

My mom died when I was a thumb-sucking five-year-old. By whatever snippets of tales I hear about her, they conclude with a mention of her skill at sustaining and cherishing relationships. When she was alive, she made sure we had scores of devoted guests.

Dad hardly spoke of her. It was mostly my aunts and

cousins who talked about her when the subject came up. I picked pieces from their stories and jigsaw-puzzled an image of her in my mind. I loved that image.

'Her relatives, or even mine for that matter, adored her and her parties. If we invited someone, they always turned up. In fact,' he says, his eyes skimming over the book he's holding but isn't reading, 'some extra people would show up and scold us for passing them over. They'd join in the party as if it were their own. All because of Mrunal.'

It is difficult for me to recollect her face at times. Just a hazy outline of her would dance in front of my eyes whenever someone mentioned her. Twelve years since she breathed her last, and I still miss her presence. Her memory, the fact that she walked on the same ground I now walk on, that she held me in her arms, that I had once looked into those dark eyes and grinned a toothless grin and that I was the reason her face lit up causes a strange warmth to flow into my heart.

'And now, for the first time, we've disappointed a person who has come to stay with us,' Dad says in the middle of my mommy daydream and I frown at him, the image of her face fading with his words.

'What are you saying?' I rest my head against the back wall and close my eyes, trying to find her face in the darkness.

Dad slaps my leg with the book. 'Don't tell me you didn't notice Cecelia wanted to go, but she was cancelling for you?'

I don't reply, mainly because my mind is focused on thoughts of my mother. I try hard, but when all I conjure up is my mom's face trapped inside a photograph, I sigh. I see her every day in old pictures, but mostly fail when I force them to come alive. I curse the memory I had as a five-year-old.

'When I first told Cecelia about this plan, she was thrilled. But the way you reacted to it, anybody would've cancelled knowing they're utterly unwelcome. She doesn't want to force her company on you. I guess you're smart enough to realize that.'

Okay, I know. Playing clueless with Dad doesn't work.

I know she is doing this for me. But I have been a bit self-seeking lately and it clouded my mind. Maybe my goodness was overpowered… if I had any at all.

'Okay.' I open my eyes. This is the least I can do to feel closer to Mom. 'I'll go.'

'*You* will go with her, but now she won't.'

'I meant I'll go apologize.'

He blinks at me before shaking his head. 'Do it if you mean it.'

And I do.

* * *

I knock on her door and poke my head in. Cecelia stands facing her closet, her back to the door.

'Please come in,' she says and I see her run her palms over her face. They stop for a second over her eyes and much to my horror, it looks like she wipes away some tears. I freeze in fright. I know I must be intolerably wrong if I have made a grown woman cry.

'I'm sorry, Aunty,' I blurt out. 'I mean, Cecelia. I'd love to go to Imagica with you.' I don't know what else to say.

'Hey, Sweety.' She smiles, gesturing for me to sit on her bed. 'What makes you think I'm cancelling this for you?' Your tears, maybe, I think nervously. 'I really have work, but I don't want to trouble your dad or his friends.'

She puts her neatly folded clothes into the left side of her closet. Her leather boots glisten on the last shelf along with red stilettos.

'I know I'm too young for this, but, um, can I help you with your presentation?' I say, studying her reaction. 'I mean I could arrange the slides and stuff. I can do that while you do the research. That way we can finish it faster. And I'm not as busy as my dad.'

She closes the cupboard doors and smiles. 'Do you think you can handle it?' She walks over and sits next to me. 'Because it is not a ten-minute presentation you have at school. It's a three-hour long corporate style demonstration.'

I chew the insides of my cheek. 'Sure, I can,' I say, quick to promise. I just hope the work won't be tedious or mind-numbing. I don't want to regret taking up this assignment. 'Maybe I'll learn a thing or two.'

'Okay. Then I will probably think about it.'

'You will?' I ask and when she nods, I sigh in relief, inviting a chuckle from her.

I hope my mom would be proud of me.

Chapter Ten

That day at lunch, Dad is quite pleased with what I did. According to him, I finally maintained some family tradition, though it had to be enforced. It somehow makes him believe I really am his daughter. He also assures me it will all be worth it, although I don't have high hopes.

Dad leans forward on the dining table when I pass him curd. 'You'd come to my room to say something in the morning?' he asks me.

I clear my mind of all its foggy thoughts and zero in on the phone conversation with Darshak. 'Oh yes!' I feel better just thinking about it. 'My friends and I are going to Prithvi Theatre tonight to watch this English comedy show about the generation gap. It's at nine o'clock.'

His face is blank. That generally means I can continue. 'Can I go?' I ask, mustering an innocent look. 'There're guys with us, too. So they will drop me home after the show.' I answer his immediate concern before he voices it. In a way, he is obliged to me as well; what with my acting like a good daughter. This is just the right time to ask for his permission.

'Cecelia, would you like to go with her? Prithvi Theatre is a must-see when you come here.'

My hand pauses halfway to my mouth.

'Every year, they hold the Prithvi Theatre Festival in

memory of Prithviraj Kapoor, India's finest actor,' he says, then looks at me as if to confirm. 'Isn't that right, dear?'

I nod slowly, narrowing my eyes at the food in front of me, wishing it would turn into a Portkey. 'In the month of November,' I add.

'Right,' he smiles. 'It wasn't a theatre first, was it? Or so I heard.'

'A travelling troupe,' I say in a monotone. 'It was a moving theatre that travelled to places in India to hold shows. Eventually, they realized they couldn't afford it and merged with another theatre company, establishing its premises here in Mumbai.'

Dad's eyes glint as he grins at me, then at Cecelia. 'It's the perfect place to start your vacation.'

He clearly doesn't notice the look I give him. Of course I can't refuse, now that I am on good terms with her. But this is all going a bit too far.

When I look at Cecelia, I see her beaming as well. 'I'd love to, especially if it's an English play,' she says and I somehow summon a broken smile to match the expressions on the two bright faces sitting across me.

* * *

In the afternoon, when Dad sleeps in his room and Cecelia in hers, I slap my pillow against my face and let out a stifled, frustrated cry. Not only have I lied to Dad about who I am going with, but I also unintentionally invited Cecelia. And moreover, the woman is on Dad's side; just her age is enough to confirm that. So, I can't possibly let her know Darshak and I are dating. She just can't get to know my secret.

I'm so knee deep in this mess that I don't even stop to think how Darshak will react to all this.

'What the hell?' he says when I narrate the whole situation to him.

I can't cancel my plan with Darshak now. It would only lead to Father getting suspicious and Cecelia would again feel bad that I'd be cancelling because of her. Though it's true, she needn't know that.

And with the girls-against-guys thing going on in our group, Divya and Purti will kill me if they find out I even considered going with Darshak in the first place. They'd never agree to come with us, so getting a bunch of friends to stick to my lie is impossible.

'I think we'll have to let her in on the secret,' Darshak says.

'What, are you insane? What if she tells on us?'

'Look, you said she is unlike the typical aunties, right? And she's a foreigner. I think she must be used to young girls having boyfriends in her country.'

He does have a point. Though not fully convinced, I give in, primarily because I can't see how else we can tackle this; also because I don't want to cancel today's plan at any cost. I'll be seeing Darshak after two whole days, so no way am I going to sacrifice meeting him for anyone else.

Chapter Eleven

'Cecelia? Are you ready yet?' I knock on her door. I want to kick it hard instead, but I don't. 'We're getting late!'

'Coming dear!' comes the accented reply.

Dad has his eyes glued to the news on the television. I glare at him and point at my watch. The seating arrangement at Prithvi Theatre is on a first-come-first-served basis. There are benches in a semi-circle in front of the stage and tickets aren't assigned to any particular bench. So we need to line up for good seats after we have been issued tickets. If we don't, we'll end up at the back or in the corners, or worse, standing.

Moreover, we don't have passes and Darshak has informed one of his friends to keep two for us. Now we need three. Online booking for the last few days has been jammed and Darshak's friend is not in any kind of authoritative position to be able to keep tickets for too long. He can only do so as long as no important folk needs them, so he had asked us to come as early as possible and claim them.

But Cecelia is taking forever to get ready. I should be the one taking longer than her, being a teenager and all.

Dad gestures for me to be patient and keep my cool. I roll my eyes at him and say if we don't get tickets, I won't think twice before blaming her. Dad tells me to do whatever

I want, but take care of Cecelia and not to board too crowded a train. She is new here. Not that she needs to be taken care of. She is old enough and nobody here has a problem understanding English, but he does his job of counselling me.

I stuff a cold water bottle into my sling bag and squeeze my feet into white sneakers.

'I'm so sorry to keep you waiting,' Cecelia says while I tie my shoelaces. I look at her feet, unable to believe someone can be that fair. Her toes peek out of red peep-toes.

She wears a black dress that falls below the knees with sleeves covering her forearms. Long earrings in her ears and a simple red bracelet on her wrist conclude her look. Her short brunette hair makes her look achingly beautiful and young. I can't help but stare.

'Nice dress, Cecelia,' my dad says and points at me. 'Teach her how to dress, as well.'

I frown. I'm wearing my faded knee-length shorts, white top and a grey jacket, hair tied up in a messy bun. The look is casual but stylish. I know I look sexy. I *feel* sexy in this outfit, but it is nothing compared to Cecelia's classy and elegant look.

Cecelia purses her lips trying not to smile at Dad's comment. I clear my throat. 'Let's move!' I say.

* * *

We take a cab to Dadar station and get down under the bridge on the west side. I open the cab door and my shoes hit a puddle. I wince and jump two steps away. I look at Cecelia through the window and gesture to her to get down from the other side.

'No change, Madam.' The cab driver twists in his seat to look at her and waves the Rs 100 she gave him in her face.

'Keep the change,' she says and starts to get out.

'What? No!' I say, reaching through the window to snatch the note from his hand. His grin turns to a scowl. I look around and take a second to decide on a shop. I run into a sweet shop, buy a Cadbury worth ten bucks and rush back to the taxi. Cecelia waits with her hand over her eyes, squinting at me through the rays of the setting sun.

'What are you doing?' she asks as I run past her to the cab and hand the driver the fare his meter displays: not more, not less.

The cab driver shoots daggers at me with his eyes and accepts the seventy bucks. Ignoring the crazy honking behind us, I hand the twenty bucks back to Cecelia.

'What was the need of that?' Cecelia asks as we make our way to the station on foot, me in front and Cecelia following close behind. 'You should've let him keep the change.'

I don't reply to her unnecessary kindness. I can see where it comes from. I remember the bag of gifts and decide it's something she can't help.

We dodge puddles, vendors and cabbage leaves that have been trampled by feet on our way into the station. The minute our feet touch the platform, my Mumbaikar instincts kick in. In the crowd of hundreds, I take a miniscule amount of time to decide which side of the crowd moves fastest and squeeze myself through the sweaty bodies all anxious to get back home and, hopefully, have a bath.

I feel a hand brush my side and linger on my backside

in the crowd. The body rubs against my back. I grit my teeth, whirl around and shoot a vicious look at a dark-skinned teenage boy walking too close behind me. The look is enough. He withdraws his hand and stiffens it beside himself. Satisfied, I match my steps in time with everyone else's.

And suddenly I stop dead in my tracks. A few people run into me and for a second, the crowd is disoriented. I see people shooting me looks as they walk around me while I stand frozen in one place. I turn around and frantically search the crowd behind me. I push past people walking in the opposite direction and get a lot of curses, a lot of people throwing, 'What the hell', at me and a lot of clicking of tongues. I get to the entrance of Dadar station and scan all the faces I set my eyes on. I run to where we got down for the cab and retrace my steps. I can't see her anywhere.

I almost flip out before my gaze falls on the fairest face there, blinking around in confusion and looking at the people walking by. Cecelia's eyes are wide and her face looks frightened. Relief washes over me. I run to where she is standing, searching through the mass of people surrounding her.

'Hey!' I say and for the first time, I find myself extremely relieved to see Cecelia in front of me. I realize it's a mutual feeling, because the minute her gaze falls on me, she clutches my hand as if it's a life jacket and she's drowning.

'Thank sweet Jesus!' she says, pulling me into a hug. I feel like a mother who'd momentarily lost her child in a mob. 'I almost lost you.'

I don't miss the fright in her voice. 'I'm so sorry,' I say hugging her back and meaning it. 'I'm so very sorry.'

We pull back but I don't let go of her arm. Cecelia glances around consciously, looking apologetic, probably for forcefully hugging me in the middle of the street and holding up people behind and around her.

Without saying a word, I pull her back into the crowd, this time holding her hand tightly in mine. I make a mental note to not let it go for the night. My dad's face flashes in front of my eyes and I thank god he isn't here to witness this.

I hear a few whistles while we walk on the foot bridge and from the corner of my eye, I find a man following us. When I narrow my eyes at him, I realize he isn't looking at us but at Cecelia—more precisely, her legs. I quicken my pace and tug her along with me, vaguely aware of her breathlessness. I decide to apologize to her later. Right now, we need to get the hell out of this place.

As we reach the platform, I see the nose of a train emerging, the crowd stepping back as if in welcome. I wait for a second for the train to arrive and my heart is in my mouth.

The ladies' compartment is empty. I glance at Cecelia, who is making an innocent effort to not dash into people and apologizing each time someone accidently bumps into her. That is a hell of a lot of times, but I don't ask her to stop.

'Can you…' I start to say and she shifts her big brown eyes to me, like she's hanging onto every word I say. Something stirs within me and as much as I hate to do it, for some absurd reason, I point at her dress, at the train and the approaching, empty ladies' compartment and say, 'We have to get into that compartment. Can you run?'

She takes one moment to think and nods. I cut through the crowd, pushing and shoving rudely, and Cecelia sticks close behind me. Seconds before the train speeds up, I push her into a compartment, supporting her back while she pulls herself in and I hop on immediately after.

We pause for a bit. Not much later, I realize I had already broken the two rules set by my dad: One, not jumping into moving trains and two, to take good care of Cecelia. These rules exclude his more pronounced, clear-cut ones that say no boyfriends or making lonely late night plans with a boy. So, today I've broken practically all his rules.

Cecelia flops onto the nearest empty seat to catch her breath. I realize we are still holding hands and so tightly, that my knuckles are almost white. I let go of her arm and watch her huff for breath, her hair is a mess and sweat is starting to break across her forehead.

I wince at the sight. I really did ruin the start of her evening. 'I'm sor—'

'That was epic!' she says beaming. My apology is stuck in my throat.

'Huh?' I didn't expect that.

She looks at me and her eyes are warm like they were when she first set them on me. 'That was *crazy*!'

I nod earnestly. 'I know.'

'And awesome, too. Something I have never experienced before.'

For a second, I think she's saying that sarcastically, but then I see her laugh.

'You aren't upset?' I take a seat next to her and look at

her in apprehension, fearing this news would reach my dad any minute.

'Of course not.' She can't seem to control her grin. 'That is one helluva experience I'll never forget. I was never lost in crowd as a kid and even if I was, I was never scared of losing sight of my parents for a while. But today?' She shakes her head as if she finds the whole thing funny, instead of nerve racking like I do.

I raise a brow when she looks at me, her face suddenly going serious. 'I'm sorry for reacting like a lost child earlier, but I kind of panicked when I paused for a second to look at that shoe shop and turned around to find you gone.' She winces at the memory, then her face relaxes. 'But it was truly fascinating. This place is crazy!' she says again. 'Guess this will be our little secret, now.'

It takes a moment for me to realize she's referring to our lost-and-found incident. I find myself smiling and it soon turns into a grin, then into uncontrollable laughter. She joins in and for a long time, we both have no clue what we're laughing at.

I see almost every single woman staring at us. I narrow my eyes at a few of them, trying to convey my discomfort at their staring. But Cecelia and I catch each other's eye and burst into another fit of giggles.

'I didn't know you could run,' I say, impressed at her swiftness. 'I mean I was mentally prepared to give up on this train.'

She shrugs. 'We were already late.'

I smile. Damn the people who are staring at us like we've escaped an asylum or something. I instinctively feel this day will be memorable.

Chapter Twelve

Two guys with gelled hair are smoking as they lean against a car parked at the mouth of the Prithvi Theatre lane. A pale girl with shiny black hair with red highlights, wearing a mid-length skirt rests her hand on the bonnet of the car. Another girl, with a comparatively darker complexion, leans against one of the guys' torsos, scrolling through her phone.

As Cecelia and I stumble and walk through the traffic and into the narrow lane, I see Darshak walking towards us with a frown. His eyes hold mine as if I am the only person he can see.

'I waited for you for an hour,' he says. Before I can explain, his gaze travels down to my hands interlocked with Cecelia's and up to her. Both of them are almost the same height.

He sizes her up in a glance. That is the only change of expression on his face. But I know that appreciative look all too well. It is reserved for me every time I look stunning... or for any other stunning girl, for that matter.

I scowl at Darshak, shooting him a look that says something like, 'Look at your girlfriend, be a good boyfriend and compliment her on her looks.' But I don't think he notices. I poke him in the stomach when Cecelia glances back to acknowledge a man asking us to excuse him.

'I think we're blocking the way,' Darshak says to Cecelia,

who apologizes to the man and steps aside, pulling me along with her. Darshak extends his hand to her. 'Hello Aunty. I'm Darshak, Neha's friend.' So he hasn't noticed my scowl. 'Most of our friends, all of them actually, dropped out because they're not feeling well. So it'll just be the three of us.'

A moment of tense silence hangs between us.

I frown, mouthing, '*What?*' to Darshak. It is probably the lamest excuse I've ever heard in my life. I shut my eyes. I know Cecelia will never buy it.

But she nods and, to my great relief, lets it pass.

'Don't call me Aunty. You can call me Cecelia.'

Darshak opens his mouth, then closes it. I know it'll be awkward for him to call a lady who is more than twice his age by her name. It is awkward for me, too.

'Okay, um, Cecelia. We'll have to wait for tickets.' He jerks his thumb in the direction of the entrance behind him. 'The theatre is full. I've asked my friend. He'll try to conjure up three tickets somehow.'

'That's okay.'

'Do you want something to eat in the meanwhile?'

'Sure.'

And they have a chat and start to walk as if I'm invisible, not that I mind. I am hungry too.

We step into Prithvi Café, a pleasantly lit open air café with a quiet, peaceful ambience. Glimmering lanterns dangle overhead and blue fairy lights wind around a tree that stands in a corner. A girl leans her back against the tree and stares into the glass of liquid in her hand. A guy next to her looks at her like he is sick to the stomach, his other hand resting on her knee.

In addition to the couple, a few people occupy tiny round tables and stools. Darshak pauses at the entrance for a second, scans the place and walks toward the far right corner with us behind him. The table we choose is comparatively longer.

An old musician with thick whiskers and short, dark hair sits to our right with a silver flute in his hand. His eyes glint under the rainbow-coloured paper lanterns hanging over his head. His hands, wrinkled and thin, quiver, but his fingers are surprisingly steady on the instrument.

As I watch him play soothing music, I ponder over which chief guest will come today. There is always one celebrity to see no matter which day we choose to visit.

'Neha, let's go order something,' Darshak says pulling me to my feet. I have to avert my eyes from the music player to pay attention to Darshak.

I ask Cecelia if she wants anything specific. She shrugs, saying I can order whatever I fancy. She hands me two Rs 500 notes, although I say I can manage. I have introduced her to an amazing place and we don't earn yet, she argues, so she'll pay.

When I smile in gratitude, she resumes staring at the flautist. Going by her expression, it seems his music has the same calming effect on her.

* * *

I walk with Darshak to the counter and stand behind the same man who'd asked us to excuse him. We wait for our turn.

'My eyes popped out the moment I saw your aunt. I

mean, who'd say she's an *aunt*!' Darshak lets out a whistle and I poke him in the ribs.

'Talk with respect, you perv. She's my aunt.'

He raises a brow, rubbing the spot where I hit him. 'Now she's your aunt, is she? I thought you didn't like her.' When I don't respond, he snorts. 'I get that you're angry I didn't look at you, but no need to hide that jealousy with fake respect for her.'

My mouth drops open. That is probably the most hurtful thing he has said to me.

I turn on my heels to face him. 'First, I'm not jealous. She's my mother's age for God's sake! And second, I don't fake respect, so back off.' I turn to the waiter who is looking at us curiously. 'Two paneer *parathas*, nachos and fries with cheese sauce, then this...' I look at the glass display and point at a chocolate dessert that has no name.

'Chocolate mousse?' The guy at the counter provides and I nod.

'And three Irish coffees.'

'That's a lot for a quick snack,' Darshak says smiling. 'But I like it when you order like you've been starved for days.' I scowl at the two Rs 500 notes in my hand.

'I'm sorry, Neha. You look beautiful tonight. Smoking hot.' Darshak clutches my elbow lightly and turns me around. His hand is icy cold. I glance at where our skins touch.

'One word, Darshak, and I'll break those perfect white teeth of yours.' I meet his gaze and hold it.

His smile dies on his face. 'You're really beautiful. And I mean, not just on the outside.'

I roll my eyes and release my arm with a tug.

'Come on, Neha. You know you look like an angel. Nevermind how Cecelia looks. She's double my age and I can't possibly flirt with her even if I wanted to.' He waves his hand. I point at him and start to say something, but he seizes my finger between his thumb and forefinger. 'But even if she were our age and a thousand times prettier than you, I would still love only you. And no matter what, I do respect your aunt.' He kisses the finger I'm pointing at him before releasing it.

The feel of his lips lingers on the tip of my finger even as I turn and wait for the waiter to assemble our order. His words resound in my ear like a melody and suddenly, I dismiss any idea that I'm supposed to stay mad.

He edges closer to me and inhales the scent of my shampoo, his nose buried in my hair... his favourite shampoo. I had washed my hair this afternoon with a purpose.

He plays with the fingers of my hand at our side, tenderly plucking at them. 'I like that colour on you, by the way,' he says close to my ear and it takes me a moment to realize he's referring to my nail paint.

My heart does a little somersault. I stop myself just in time before I can whirl around and ask, 'You noticed?' Instead, I simply glance at him out of the corner of my eye and thank him.

'Stop hiding your smile and faking anger. I can read your face better than a book,' he says, taking a step back, creating a void between us. My heart sinks. I liked him better close. 'But why exactly are you so annoyed in the first place? You didn't possibly think I liked your aunty that way, did you?'

I slide the money on the counter towards the waiter as Darshak takes the tray from his hand. I don't have a specific reason to pin point. It is more a series of events that led to it.

'I've been mad since the evening,' I explain. 'First, Cecelia was uninvited, then late. Then people ogled her all the way, but she was so oblivious to everyone. They whistled and commented in Hindi. It kind of pissed me off.' I ball my fists. 'I'd have trashed those perverts, you know? They looked at her like she was a piece of meat.'

I sigh. 'And then when I come here, the first thing you say is that she is sexy. I mean, give her a break, you guys.'

'Relax, fighter. I was just appreciating her beauty. I had no other thoughts running through my mind, except marvelling at how she has maintained herself.' He loops his free arm around my neck. 'And anyway, those kinds of thoughts are only reserved for one person in this world.' I scuttle away from his grip and shake my head.

We're laughing when someone calls Darshak's name. We turn our heads in the direction of the voice. 'I think the tickets are available.' Darshak hands me the tray and starts towards his friend.

'Wait! I'll come, too,' I thrust the tray into the hands of a waiter standing close by and ask him to put it on our table. I send a message to Cecelia saying that we'd be back with tickets in no time.

Chapter Thirteen

'Sorry, bro.' His friend drives us into a corner and runs his hand through his hair. 'No passes. I tried everything.'

A gasp escapes my mouth. Before we can say anything, another guy walks over to Darshak's friend, grabs his arm and whispers something in his ear. Darshak's friend looks at the other guy, his eyes going wide. 'Already?'

The other guy nods.

'Okay. I'll be there. And hey,' he pulls back the guy hurrying away. 'Do you have any extras left?'

The guy taps his jacket pocket. 'Taken,' he says.

'I'm sorry.' Darshak's friend turns to us and grimaces. 'I'm extremely sorry. It's just that the queue was already too long and many people have left empty-handed. You should have come a little early.'

What? Now we just go back home? No, this is not done. We come all the way here, overcoming all the odds and then we hear this.

'Do you think there will be any cancellations within the next hour?'

'I don't think so.' He glances around impatiently, like he can't wait to get away from us. I don't like him. 'You both wait here. I'll send the lady who is in charge of handing out the passes. Cook up a story and tell her it's really important that you watch this show, it's for a college assignment and you will fail if you don't watch it. Act it out. See if you can convince her.'

I have barely ever seen a theatre where the audience has to beg for tickets. But I am ready to do whatever is necessary. I won't let my trip go to waste.

As we wait for the lady for over half an hour, I look at Darshak for the first time since we met that day. Like, *really* look. He wears knee-length jeans fashionably torn at the knee and a green, full-sleeved jacket. He has his black headphones hanging loosely round his neck and a thin bracelet on his left wrist.

'You look handsome,' I murmur, without letting him know I am smitten. Yet again. He grins, slips his hand into mine and we are quiet while we wait for the lady.

* * *

Shoulders hunched and feeling defeated, we walk back to our table. Darshak hasn't said a single word since we had argued with and begged the lady-in-charge to let us in. She had eventually waved her hand and had started to walk away, visibly shooing us. His shoulders are stiff and jaw tight as he walks alongside me. If you look closely, you can see his temple throb.

He must feel more miserable than I do. He couldn't stand by his word. I don't say anything. The last thing I want is to blame him and hurt his wounded ego.

'It's okay,' I say a few times, trying to comfort him. 'We'll come some other time.'

He frowns. If it was just the two of us, we'd have driven to the nearest eatery, gorged on chicken and then maybe would have found a quiet place and snuggled depending on our moods. It wouldn't have mattered all that much what we did as long as I was back home by the time the show ended. But now a third member is involved.

When we are a few steps away from our table I skid to a halt, causing Darshak to jerk to a stop as well. He clicks his tongue and follows my gaze. His eyes bulge out, just as my mouth has dropped open. I stand there transfixed for a few seconds before I'm able to collect my thoughts.

* * *

Cecelia is sitting with Genelia Deshmukh, the famous Bollywood actress and with them is her husband. I see Cecelia throw her head back and laugh, as if she has known them forever. Riteish Deshmukh's mouth forms an adorable smile. Genelia takes another sip from my Irish coffee and pops a nacho into her mouth.

I force my feet to move. When we stand next to their table, hesitant and charmed, Cecelia turns to us. 'Here they are!' she says and rises to her feet. 'This is Neha. The girl I was talking about.'

'Hello there, gorgeous.' Riteish Deshmukh extends his hand to me. I lurch forward to take it, hitting my elbow on the table in my haste.

'Relax. We're not running away,' he comments and the two women giggle.

'Hello,' I say staring at his beautiful face. I look at Genelia and her eyes are warm.

'And here's Darshak, her friend.'

'Young man,' Riteish says, as they shake hands. Darshak opens his mouth but no words come out. Going by his expression, he looks as though he might not speak for the next few days.

Cecelia tugs her stool into a corner and Darshak and I exchange glances as we sit in front of the couple as graciously as we can.

'So did you get the tickets?' Cecelia turns to face us.

I shake my head. 'It's full,' I say and see Darshak shrink in his seat.

'Oh that's fine! I think these wonderful people will help us.' She gestures to the star couple.

'Of course,' Genelia slurps the last bit of her coffee and nods. She places her empty mug on the table and smiles at us. 'It'd be a pleasure to make sure your guest watches an Indian play. And anyway,' she says, 'I wondered how you could manage to get tickets at this hour. It's next to impossible.'

Darshak raises his head and I nod, urging her to keep talking.

'I will make arrangements for the three of you.' Genelia pulls her phone out and swipes on a name. Within the next ten minutes, we have three tickets waiting for us at the entrance.

* * *

Darshak gropes around under the table and I jerk when his fingers touch my knee.

'Are you fine?' Cecelia asks. I had interrupted their discussion about George Clooney. I nod and when she turns back to make a point, I widen my eyes at Darshak. What is he doing? This is not the time OR the place.

But he isn't looking at me. His attention is fixed on the conversation, his hand groping my thigh. I slap my palm over his hand to stop him. Instantly, he pushes money into it and pulls it back.

Genelia slides an untouched glass of Irish coffee in front of me. Other than that, only a nacho and a sad *paratha* lie on our plates.

'Sorry, we finished everything.' Genelia shrugs sheepishly. 'We hadn't had anything since afternoon. I wanted to grab a snack before they could pull us back into the crowd,' she says. 'It's funny how often people forget we're humans too. So I'm glad Riteish found you.' She looks over at her husband and smiles. 'And at just the right time, right?'

We wait for Riteish to toss in a clever retort. He pops the lone nacho into his mouth and smirks. 'Why do you think I introduced myself?' He licks the tip of his finger. I giggle along with the others, now thoroughly charmed by how down to earth both of them are.

And then I jerk up again, this time at Darshak's kick.

Before I can shoot him a vicious look, he speaks without waiting for me to understand the reason for his assaults. 'Sorry to interrupt, but can we know how much the tickets cost?' A moment of collective silence follows his words. All eyes are on him, waiting for him to say more. 'So we can pay you,' he explains.

I glance down at the three Rs 500 notes in my hand. He asked me to ask them about the money.

Right. How could I have forgotten that?

Genelia raises her perfectly shaped eyebrows.

'Brother, I'd rather have you watch our films than pay us back,' Riteish says, trying to hide a smile. 'Besides we paid for your tickets; you paid for our pre-dinner snacking.' His soft eyes shine with mischief. '*Ho gaya hisaab*?' (Are all the debts settled?) Darshak starts to shake his head, his face flushed. 'Relax, young man. I'm joking,' he says, interrupting whatever Darshak was about to say. 'And they are free for us. Perks of being a producer,' he winks.

After about five more minutes of chatting, where all I do is stare at how Genelia's pearly white teeth shine each time she smiles and how Riteish's lips turn up at the corner before he tosses out a pun, a few people come asking for their chief guests.

When the couple rises to leave, they shake hands with Cecelia. 'Nice knowing you,' Genelia says. 'Tell me how you liked the show.'

'Most definitely. And I'll write you a nice long review about your movie.' They exchange personal email-ids.

Darshak's friend stands in the mob of around seven to eight people and when he sees us talking to his chief guests, his face goes white as if he's seen a ghost. I raise my chin in his general direction, trying to convey that we are not at his mercy anymore. If he couldn't help us, we called upon higher authorities to arrange for passes.

By a stroke of luck, maybe, but we did.

Riteish blinks at me once and smiles before disappearing into the crowd. I grin back like an idiot, realizing I could stare at his face all day and never get bored.

I also realize I have just developed a full-blown crush on that man.

We watch them vanish into the crowd and inside the theatre. Going by Darshak's look, he is equally mesmerized by the entire encounter. But he's still in his senses, unlike me, because the minute the place is quiet and back to normal he says, 'I'll go, order two more coffees.'

When we are left by ourselves, I slump in my seat and look at Cecelia as if I am seeing her for the first time.

Chapter Fourteen

'What in the world was that?' I ask her. 'Did you know them?'

'Before today? No.'

I cross my arms and look at her. 'I wanna hear this from the beginning.'

We wait for Darshak to return and when he does, Cecelia says, 'To start with, I sat here waiting for you and listening to the soothing instrument that man was playing.' She nods towards the old man, his fingers moving over the flute, his eyes shut.

'Flute,' I provide.

'Yeah.' Cecelia rubs her arms to warm them. 'And you were taking too long. I had nothing better to do, so I talked with him.'

'To the flautist?' I lift my head and catch sight of him behind her. He looks engrossed. I did not see him steal a glance at the star couple even once. As if their presence a few centimetres away from him was a regular occurrence in his life.

Which perhaps, I realize, it is; or maybe, he is the world's most loyal employee. Like Dad says, every person is the world's most loyal employee as long as he works for his passion, not his pension.

So the story is that Cecelia had asked the man about the instrument: Where had he got it, where had he learned to play it, how long had it taken him to master it, whether he played by ear or if he had learnt to read music and which one was easier? Just making small talk.

Riteish had stood a few feet away, talking to some corporate lad. He had darted occasional glances towards Cecelia and the old man.

After she had pestered the flautist for fifteen minutes, he had got annoyed with her. When she had asked him one particular question about the number and kinds of flutes in the world, he had snapped at her.

'Madam, will you please let me do my job?' Cecelia imitates his Indian accent and I choke with laughter.

She had apologized to him, but she had been embarrassed. A few people sitting close by had sniggered at her. Seeing Cecelia hang her head and take a quiet sip of her Irish coffee attempting to brush off the remarks, Riteish had excused himself from the lad and had asked Cecelia if he could sit next to her.

'You mean *the* Riteish Deshmukh,' I say. It isn't a question.

'Yes.' She drops her hand into her lap and shrugs.

She hadn't known who the man was, but he had looked decent and kind, so she had let him sit with her. He had taken a seat opposite her and had answered whatever she had asked the flautist. He had also apologized for the man's rudeness and for the other Indians mocking her curiosity.

'He did?'

'He's a gentleman.'

'He is,' I say and see Darshak roll his eyes beside me. My crush on the man has just grown.

A while later, Genelia had walked in escorted by two men, one on either side of her. She had hesitated at the table where Riteish had been sitting and had smiled tentatively at Cecelia. Riteish had pulled her into the seat next to him and had asked her escorts to return in some time.

Cecelia had offered them the food we had sent. Riteish had said he wasn't a shy guy and had dived in while his wife had widened her eyes at him. When Cecelia had pressed her, she had dug in too.

'I had no clue they were top Bollywood actors and the chief guests today until people started to come up to greet them,' Cecelia says. 'I'm glad to have met them.'

'So are we,' I grin and Darshak nods. His posture and facial muscles appear more relaxed than they did before.

Cecelia had told the couple the reason for her visit to India, where she was staying and more. She had also assured them we'd get tickets. That was when Genelia had voiced her concern and had offered to help if we didn't. She had updated Cecelia about her upcoming projects. Riteish had joked he had a thing for Christian women whose name ended in 'lia'; and he had found himself meeting precisely those women. I chuckle.

'He's funny, that man,' Cecelia says, settling back in her seat.

I let out a breath. This is all too much for one day.

I see Darshak cast a glance behind me and raise his hand. 'Order's ready,' he says to us, grabs my purse from the table, pulls out some cash and strides off. I watch him walk away, taking quick long strides, his hands swinging at his sides. They almost look rhythmic, his movements, like poetry in motion.

'Good choice,' Cecelia nudges me. 'He isn't too bad for a boyfriend.'

I freeze, suddenly aware of her presence beside me. When I turn to her, I find her scrutinising me. 'What do you mean?'

She nods towards Darshak. 'Him,' she says, smiling, her chin resting on her palm casually. 'You. Good enough.'

'How,' I look down, embarrassed, 'how do you know?'

'Easy. You wouldn't panic for no reason at the prospect of having someone accompany you. And think about it. Would *you* believe it if someone told you their friends dropped out of a plan at the last moment for some illness and now it is just the two of you?' She crosses her hands on the table. 'It was not a very believable excuse.'

Fear creeps into the pit of my stomach. Darshak had all day to think of an excuse and what does he come up with? Everybody dropped out because of fever; all six friends falling sick at the same time.

Poetry in motion or not, he was a bum.

I know I'm risking it, but now that my secret is out I might as well let her in. 'You won't tell Papa, will you?'

Crossing her heart, she mimes zipping her mouth. I smile.

When Darshak returns with our sandwiches, we gorge on them. After an hour, we cross the threshold of the theatre filled with an enthusiastic public and watch the show till the end, sitting in the very reserved VIP seats.

Chapter Fifteen

The next evening I know Dad and Cecelia are preparing for that important meeting Cecelia flew in from Canada for. So they're both going to stay in the office for the whole evening and the night along with the team. Since they won't be home for tonight, Dad asks me about a dozen times if I'll be fine.

'Papa, looks like you have a little problem remembering facts. You were gone for three years and I lived without you every night.' The look on his face makes my heart sink.

'I wouldn't have gone if I didn't have work,' he says, getting defensive.

'Of course, I know,' I rush to add. 'But that is not the point. The point is if I can live three crucial years of my teen life alone, one more night won't be any different, will it?'

He furrows his bushy brows. 'You had Nani with you back then.'

'Nani.' I smile, shaking my head. 'A woman who can't hear unless you're shouting in her ears and has a problem telling who's who if you're standing farther than five feet away.'

'Neha.' Dad's voice is curt. 'She's your Nani. Be respectful.'

'Sorry.' I hold my hands up. 'I love her more than anyone on this planet. But you get the point? I'll be *fine*. Now go get ready for the big day.'

His face is thoughtful. Cecelia sits across from us while I try to convince Dad he needn't worry so much. She notices the look on Dad's face too, because in my defence she says, 'I believe her. You shouldn't fret so much. She's a big girl now.'

'Thank you.'

'Sure you'll be fine?'

'Cross my heart.' I wink at Cecelia who smiles, understanding the reference.

Dad sighs, but his face visibly relaxes. 'Okay.' He kisses the top of my head and turns to Cecelia. 'Geeta and Bob will pick you up in two hours. I'll get going now.'

'Sure.'

As one of the leaders of their construction project, Dad needs to reach office early, so he can discuss survey reports, costs, design and other planning details about their project in a meeting, make pointers and then communicate them to the others. Cecelia says she'll accompany him, but she'll be waiting for god knows how many hours. So she is better off going with Bob Uncle and Geeta Aunty in their car, while Dad drives to the office first.

All in all, I now have two hours until she leaves. I'm especially looking forward to it, so I can do what I've been planning to for days.

Cecelia gets to her feet when Dad is out the door. 'I'll go take a shower.'

'Sure.' I watch her go in and hear the guest room door lock.

Finally!

Relieved, I pick up my cell phone and call Darshak.

'What the hell, Neha? How long are you going to take?' he asks, his voice tinged with irritation.

'Sorry, Babu. I'll come as quickly as I can get rid of Cecelia.'

'She hasn't left yet?'

'No. There is a change in plan, but she will leave soon,' I say, forcing enthusiasm into my voice. 'In about two hours.' I close my eyes and wait for the outburst.

'Two fucking hours!'

'Shush! Stop shouting.'

He groans. 'I think we should just chuck this plan.'

'No!' I gasp. 'Just two more hours and I'll meet you at CCD, okay? I love you.'

This was my plan. Our last date had been three months ago to a flop movie, where all we did was stare ahead in silence and eat popcorn with Darshak dozing off sometime before the climax. I wanted conversations and I was dying to go on a real date with him again.

And what's better than a long drive along Marine Drive after sunset? Since Dad doesn't usually allow anything that remotely involves late nights, I thought this was an ideal way of sneaking out for alone time. Some spicy snacks at Chowpatty, some time by the beach followed by a drive along the Queen's Necklace. And knowing how Darshak is perpetually ready for long drives, especially when I sit behind snuggling closer to him, he didn't oppose the idea either.

The only hitch is that Darshak is already at CCD waiting for me to arrive. We decided to sneak out by seven. But now it's been an hour since Dad left and I'm still home, waiting for Cecelia to get going. As much as I feel bad for making Darshak wait, I'm doing the same, only at home.

'Nay-ha.' I nearly jump out of my skin when the sound of my name interrupts my thoughts. 'Sorry, didn't mean to scare you.'

I stare at her, my heart pounding loudly in my chest. She's chewing her bottom lip and her face doesn't look as friendly as it did two minutes ago. A thought crosses my mind and my heart beats fast with nervousness. Did she hear me?

'Can I have some body wash?' she says. Her voice is distant and emotionless.

'Yeah sure,' I respond and get to my feet. I scuttle around my bathroom and hand her a Palmolive body wash, avoiding eye contact.

'Thanks,' she replies, but doesn't move.

I don't dare look at her eyes, fearing I might see something in them I don't want to. So I turn around and start to go back to the living room when I hear her voice.

'Don't do it.'

I stop in my tracks. She heard me. Shit. Shit. Shit.

'What?' I surprise myself when my voice comes out steady and guiltless.

'You know what.' We are both quiet for a long time, each waiting for the other to say something. She speaks up first. 'Your dad trusts you.'

I want to ask her, 'So?' It's not like he'd know I was breaking his trust behind his back... unless someone tells him.

'Cecelia.' It still feels odd to call her by her name, but that's the least of my concerns right now. 'I'm sorry you heard me, but if you want to change my mind, that's not possible. And if you want to tell my dad, go ahead.'

Please say no. Please say no. Please say no.

'Who told you I'd tell Mr Ranade?' I sigh with relief, but it doesn't end there. 'I didn't tell him about you having a boyfriend and I won't tell him this. I'm just trying to warn you...'

'*Warn* me?' I whirl to face her and my voice has an edge of frustration. Who the hell is she to warn me? 'You know what? If you think you can use this tactic and get into my good books or whatever then that's a little difficult. I know you're trying hard and I appreciate it. But really, I'd rather have you as a temporary guest than my supposed friend poking your nose into my business every now and then.'

She frowns. 'Interfering was never my intention. I just care about you.' I roll my eyes. 'I don't want anything happening to you and then seeing Mr Ranade get all worked up.'

'He wouldn't if he doesn't know. And I've been on such drives before. It's Mumbai, busy twenty four-seven, so I'll be fine.'

She stares at me and shakes her head. 'I'd still think twice.'

'I already have.' If I'm confident and stubborn, she'll let it pass, I tell myself. 'And you can blackmail me if you want, but that isn't going to change my decision. I've been used to living my life on my terms when Dad was here and also when he wasn't. And I don't plan on changing that for someone who's come into this house like a hurricane.' Temporary and unwanted is what I don't add.

She stares at me quietly for a moment. 'Hope you have a safe whatever you're going to have,' she says and with that, she walks into her room. 'And you don't have to wait to get rid of me. You are free to do whatever!' she snaps, banging the door shut practically in my face.

I sigh. I don't really blame her.

Chapter Sixteen

What I do next is probably the rudest thing I've ever done. I go to my room, change into my jeans and the crop top I had laid out on my bed for this night, iron out my fringe and sling my bag over my shoulder before walking out of my room. I find Cecelia in the living room, wearing an ironed black blazer over a snow white shirt and pants and waiting for her pick up to arrive. Her short hair is loose and well set. A touch of light makeup seems to have smoothened out her wrinkles. She looks breathtaking in her formals, but I don't mention it to her.

As I pass through the living room to get to the main door, she glances up at me and our eyes meet. She quickly averts hers, looking down at the book in her hand.

'I'm leaving,' I tell her. All I get in return is silence, but I can tell she's hanging onto my every word. Her jaw is set and she frowns at a point in the book without blinking or moving her eyes. 'I'll be with Darshak. We'll eat dinner at Chowpatty, take a long drive along Marine Drive and he'll drop me home. I'll be back before midnight and I'll make sure I'm safe.'

I wait for her to say something. When she doesn't, I sigh and open the main door.

'Please don't,' she says. She's on her feet and is staring at me with hard eyes. 'I'm telling you—'

'See ya,' I say and I'm out the door before she has a chance to change my mind.

* * *

Guilt tugs at my heart and I almost turn around to go back home, but then I see Darshak's bike parked outside CCD. Through the glass windows, I see him scrolling through his phone, which is in one hand. He's holding a coffee mug in the other. I burst through the door and practically announce my arrival. The moment our eyes meet, his face splits into a grin and I know I've made the right decision.

Darshak peeks at his wristwatch and then at me. 'I thought you said you'd take two hours.'

I shrug. 'Surprise.'

He leans back in his chair and runs his hand through his hair. The unmistakable joy on his face makes me want to hold his face and plant a kiss on his smile. And I do, much to the surprise of a few people sitting around.

'Wow,' he says and his smile widens. 'Thanks.'

I take his coffee and have a generous sip.

'Cecelia left?' he asks.

I nod stiffly.

'Good. Let's get going, then.'

* * *

In the next half an hour, driving through late evening traffic, we reach Chowpatty and enjoy the breezy weather. It's almost dark now at 8:30 p.m. and I guess Bob Uncle and Geeta Aunty must have picked Cecelia up. They must be on their way to the office.

Darshak offers me candy floss and I realize my mind has been lingering on Cecelia and on what she must be doing the whole time. I don't even remember Darshak asking me if I want to eat something.

I need to shove her out of my thoughts. This is not the time to feel guilty or worry about her. She'll forget about me when she reaches office and buries herself in her work. Dad must be almost done with his meeting. He must be waiting for the others to come so he can start the work.

Maybe I should call him and ask if she's reached?

'What did you think of me first when you saw me?' Darshak asks, sitting cross legged on the sand, licking the candy floss off his fingertips.

'I...' I need to stop. This was one thing I had wanted to do for as long as I can remember. Spending time with him and not have anything or anyone bother us, not even in my thoughts. Now that I have this, I should enjoy it.

I force my mind back to us and look at him. His eyes are waiting for me. I see a piece of candyfloss stuck to his right cheek. 'When I first saw you,' I say, gingerly brushing it off, 'I thought you were a total, pompous ass.'

'Shut it.' He grins. 'I know you were smitten by me.'

Well, he isn't exactly wrong.

* * *

When I first took admission in this junior college, I sat alone on a bench on the first day of classes. Just out of school, I was as lost as one could get. I remember changing my top five times before I settled on wearing the one I had first plucked out of my wardrobe. It was a long, peach top with little black hearts on it.

I had chosen to sit on the third last bench and watched as students started to pour in, everyone choosing to sit on a separate bench and hoping someone would decide to sit next to them. The class had been silent, like a graveyard. Occasional polite whispers of, 'What's your name?' and 'When do you think the class will start?' had drifted about.

That was when a girl had launched herself into the seat next to me. She had sighed, said something about the elevators not working and how stairs were her enemy, too.

'Why can't they make escalators?' she had asked, glancing over at me as if I were in charge of the college infrastructure. 'Or at least, take care of the lifts? I think we pay enough to build one in a working condition.'

I had nodded earnestly. 'I think so, too.'

And with that, our conversation had ended… Partly because my attention was directed to the front of the class. Darshak had entered with his bag hanging loosely over one shoulder. I had glanced around and had noticed a few girls stealing glances at him. He wasn't the best looking guy, but there was something about him that made you look twice.

Now I know what that is—confidence and an easy stage presence.

'He's hot, isn't he?' Purti had wriggled her brows at me and I had flushed, hating myself the moment I did.

Our friendship wasn't anything extraordinary. We met, exchanged numbers, chatted and our friendship developed. But the moment all three of us had registered for the college fest that year—Purti and Darshak for solo singing and myself for anything and everything that didn't require talent or being in front of huge crowds—was the moment our friendship had grown stronger.

Our friends and seniors, who were searching for a temporary keyboard player and for singers, had loved Darshak's stage presence and had said they'd work on his voice. Purti had hit the first note and her place in the band had been finalized. I had noted down names of shortlisted artists.

I remember Shirish asking me to read out the names of people he'd selected and I had hesitated at Darshak's name. I had desperately wanted him to get in and had practically jumped like a kangaroo around my seniors promoting Purti and Darshak.

I had persuaded the seniors into seeing the future, bright and achievable. Imagine how easily Darshak would lead the musicians and Purti would captivate everyone with her powerful, high-pitched voice. Finally, they had waved their hands and agreed. I don't know whether they had really liked them or just obliged to shut me up, but that had been the start of our new bond.

When Darshak had learnt how I had put my foot down and insisted he be in the band, I had melted with embarrassment. But he had smiled and nodded thanks to me.

Six months later, he had said he loved me in a café where I was devouring an extra-large burger, much too huge for my mouth. I had been so stunned I couldn't speak for a minute.

And like an idiot, I had asked him why, instead of just saying I loved him too and shutting up.

'You supported me when you didn't even know me

personally. Imagine how much you'll support me when we're actually together.'

That had been his explanation for saying he loved me. I frowned at it, but I'd have bought any reason, really. Even if he'd said I was the last girl on the planet and he had no other choice.

I had tossed back the four words and we were forced to pay the bills for everyone that afternoon.

Chapter Seventeen

'What did you think of me?' I ask him while we sit in the sand.

'First, I didn't even notice you and I'm just being honest. You were just another girl to me. But then I saw you working your ass off just to make our band performance a success in my first year with them,' Darshak says. 'I mean, I saw your ass first, then how you worked it off.'

I punch his arm.

'But I was a little nervous,' he admits, smiling. 'And the way you comforted me, I think I started to like you then. And then when I learnt you were one of the reasons why I was selected, I was a goner.'

I smile, in a way flattered that he remembers all that. I loop my hand in his and rest my head on his shoulder. After about another half an hour, we eat till our pockets are almost empty and stomachs full, and finally, do what we've come here to do.

We take a long U-turn so we can ride the bike back towards Chowpatty and watch the radiant beauty of Queen's Necklace from as close as we can get. I take off the scarf tied across my mouth and let the wind tease my hair. I close my eyes and the cool wind that makes me shiver feels awfully liberating.

'So chilled!' I say and pull my shoulder in so I can fit behind Darshak's frame. Darshak straightens in his seat so his body hides me from the harsh, direct gusts of wind. I wrap my hands around him, squeezing his inflated jacket.

It's about 10:00 p.m. now. We drive for another fifteen minutes and wait for a signal to turn green, when I rest my chin on his shoulder and say, 'Darshak, I want to drive.'

He looks at me through his helmet's visor and shakes his head.

'Please. Just once. In an area that's not very crowded.'

He doesn't reply.

'You know I can drive a two-wheeler.' My voice is almost pleading. 'I'll go very slow. And I remember all your lessons.' Last year, he taught me the basics of riding a bike and I drove half a kilometre in a straight line, if that counts as experience.

The signal turns green and he starts the bike.

'Please?' I say and am met with his silence. We're about two signals ahead and he still hasn't showed any signs of handing me the vehicle. I sigh and bury my face in his jacket.

A few minutes later, Darshak takes a right turn, parking in a lane that's quiet and breezy. He pulls his helmet off and slaps my leg. 'Get down.'

I do. He gets off the bike and pushes the helmet toward me. I take it like it's a newborn baby and stare at him, my eyes wide. 'Really?'

He gestures to his bike in an old-fashioned 'ladies first' sort of way and I squeak. I pull the helmet over my head and wait for him to get on the bike. His hands reach over mine to steady the bike while he mounts it and pushes the stand up. The moment it's up, I grab the handle bars tighter, keeping the beast balanced. I had forgotten how heavy this thing was.

I twist the key once in the ignition and a few lights show up on the dashboard in front of me. I press the starter button. The bike growls for a second and goes silent. I press the starter button twice more.

'Darshak?' I call softly, wanting to make sure he's still behind me.

'Hmm,' he says, sounding bored.

'Are you not gonna help?'

'I thought you said you remembered all my instructions.' He brushes the hair on my shoulder, balling it into a knot behind my back. 'If you don't, then you can get back.'

'No!' I say and clutch the handle bars tighter, if that's possible, fearing it might be taken away. I hear him chuckle.

'Then start it and ride.'

Now that I'm sure I'm not getting any help, I take a deep breath and trace back to my lessons. I kick start the bike, rev the engine and the sudden roaring sound makes my heart race. I squeeze the clutch and keep my fingers wrapped lightly around the throttle.

I shift to first gear, ignoring the sweat starting to break across my palms. I release the clutch gradually, turn the throttle and we move several inches forward against the wind.

I hear my own heartbeat, loud and pounding, and I'm beaming from ear to ear. The fact that Darshak isn't saying anything gives me strength. That means I must be doing it right.

The bike moves slowly, but the speed doesn't matter; the fact that I'm riding it does. I reach the main road in about a minute and stop at the turn. Darshak's legs are on the ground first.

'What happened?'

'This is the main road,' I say.

'So? You don't want to ride anymore?'

'I...' I thought this ride would last until I reached the end of this lane and I wouldn't be allowed farther than that. But Darshak doesn't sound like he'd meant to give me a baby ride. The moment I realize this, I can't contain my smile. 'Can I?'

'If you can.'

'Thank you!' I say and start the bike again. I make sure I drive to the side of the road, so I don't hold up traffic and don't have to speed up too much.

'If you maintain this speed, I think we'll reach home tomorrow,' Darshak says and hugs my stomach. 'But I like it like this.'

'Don't move!' I say stiffening up. When he steadies himself, I shift the bike to third gear.

He looks over my shoulder and makes funny sounds. 'Mmm. I like this.' He laughs when a girl on a Pep Plus overtakes us. But I don't focus on that. Instead, my attention is divided between the road and Darshak's hot breath on my bare shoulder. It's distracting. I can't imagine how he handles my tickling and resting against his back whenever *he's* riding the bike.

When I start to tell him to sit back, he plants a kiss on my shoulder and I sigh. It isn't until I see a hand waving in front of me that I realize who it is and jerk my shoulder.

'What?' Darshak asks, irritated. I slow down the bike and gesture to the person standing in front of us, now only about a foot away. Darshak's hand is placed lightly on my right shoulder. I guess he sees the man with the stoic expression on his face as well. His grip tightens on my arm.

I cut the engine and Darshak's foot is on the ground first. My palms feel sore and shaky. I curse inside the helmet, safe in the knowledge that the big, shadowy man towering over our bike can't hear me.

'What is going on?' The cop covers the distance between us in two big steps and pulls out a notepad from his shirt pocket.

I pull off my helmet. The policeman looks at Darshak pointedly, who is now sitting upright in his seat. We have both gone silent. The cop takes one look at us and says,

'Show me the documents and licence.'

Darshak and I get off the bike. Darshak pulls out the registration, PUC and insurance papers from the under-seat storage and hands it to the cop. After scanning them thoroughly, the cop hands them back and says, 'Show me your licence.'

Darshak starts to reach into his pocket.

'Not you.' The cop points the tip of his pen at me. 'Yours.'

'I...' I look at Darshak for help.

'Here is mine.' Darshak pushes his licence forward, literally into the man's face and the man scowls at him.

'You don't understand what I say?' He swats Darshak's hand away. 'I am asking for her licence.'

'I don't have it.' I say honestly.

'Driving without licence.' He nods, sounding not in the least bit surprised. He probably expected it. A satisfied sneer touches his lips for a second as he scribbles something on his notepad and then caps his pen. 'Come to the police station.'

The warmth I felt inside when Darshak snuggled closer to me while riding the bike is replaced by fear. I'm suddenly aware of how cold this night is.

'Sir, we're sorry. Extremely. Can we solve this here?'

The cop, Athvale his name tag reads, stares at Darshak with a brooding, superior look. He starts to open his mouth, but another cop joins him, the one that has been watching us from a distance. I squirm under their stares. I tug at my crop top wishing it would cover the thin strip of my waist line that peeks out from under its hem.

'Look what days have come? Little kids like you have started using such words,' Athvale tells his colleague. 'They don't have licence. This girl was driving on road and the boy was kissing her. In broad daylight. Now they want to bribe us. No manners, no shame.'

I almost start to correct him—its night time, not day—but decide against it. Correcting him is the last thing that will help our situation right now.

'Take them to the station. These type of kids are not supposed to get away easily,' the other cop says and we don't have any choice but to follow them.

Chapter Eighteen

As we make our way to the police station, Darshak hands me his jacket. Without a word, I slide into it and zip it up to my collar bone. We take two seats in front of Athvale at the station and he starts to interrogate us: where we live, our names, our families, college names. He makes us take the alcohol test as well, which only makes me want to shrink in my seat.

Fifteen minutes later, we have done everything in our power—pleaded, apologized, offered bribes and asked to go home and bring my licence—but nothing we say satisfies them.

'Call your parents,' he says as a twisted last option. 'Only then I'll let you go.'

Both our faces go white at this unexpected demand. I want the earth to open up and swallow me whole.

'What? Pissed in your pants?' The cop directs his glare at Darshak who looks more scared than I do at the prospect of bringing his parents into this. 'Call them. They should know what their kids are up to nowadays. Do they know you're here?'

'But...' Darshak starts and I clutch his hand to stop him from saying anything. Enough of this torture.

'Yes, they do.'

The cop slowly shifts his gaze to me. He's been merciful

towards me, not directing his harsh words or insults my way, asking me questions a little more politely. But I can't stand Darshak being targeted, especially seeing that he has done nothing wrong. Besides, I don't escape the cop's judgemental eyes that strip us both naked.

'They do? Then you shouldn't have a problem calling them here.'

Darshak starts to open his mouth, but I stop him again. I switch my phone on and dial the first number that comes to my mind.

'Cecelia...' I say, my voice shaking. Darshak holds my hand tight and that is the only way I keep from breaking. 'I'm...' I lower my voice, so the cop sitting in front of us doesn't have the benefit of hearing my every word. 'I'm sorry I didn't listen to you. I... I need your help.'

'Wait,' she says and there are noise fluctuations on the line. I hear scraping noises, a door being opened and then shut. 'Where are you?'

'At Marine Drive police station.'

'What?'

'We... I was driving a bike without a license. And we don't have enough money to pay the fine.'

'Oh god.'

'I'm so sorry. I know you're in—'

'How long have you been there?'

'About half an hour now,' I say, my voice so small I can barely hear it myself.

'Where is this licence of yours?'

'In my purple purse on the dressing table.'

There's a silence. It looks like she has put me on mute, but then I hear her talking to someone.

'Yeah, well my mum is... needs me... I don't know how she can...' she's saying, her words sound distant and muffled. I strain my ears to catch them.

'But we can do that tomorrow morning as soon as we get home.'

Father.

My heart sinks while I wait for their barely audible conversation to end.

'No, I'll manage... Maybe...'

'Okay. Call me as soon as you...'

It isn't until Cecelia is back on the line that I realize I've been holding my breath. 'I'll call you when I reach home,' she says to me. I hear her ragged breath and fast footsteps. She is running, I can tell.

I close my eyes to stop the stinging behind them. 'I'm...' I don't recognize my voice. It's just a whisper. I want to apologize to her, thank her, hug her. If I could, I'd kiss her feet right now.

'Later,' she says and the line is cut.

* * *

An hour later while we wait inside an empty cell—yes, they put us in a cell—I see Cecelia rush in through the door. The cell door isn't locked and we still have our phones and I have my purse. It's only that they didn't have a place for us to sit, so they turned a prison cell into a makeshift sitting area. The irony of the situation makes me dizzy.

When my eyes fall on her, I can't believe I'm looking at the same person I saw in the evening. Her hair is bathed in sweat, the shirt that was elegantly tucked into her pants now hangs loose over it and her heels are peeking out of her bag. She's wearing my sneakers.

Darshak and I are both on our feet. Cecelia takes out my licence and slaps it in front of the cop she sees first. She looks around searching for us and I wave my hand at her. When her eyes find mine, she doesn't smile, just nods. I want to go and hug her, but I don't. Not yet.

We both join her without saying a word. We take our seats in front of the cop who scans my licence with laser-sharp eyes, with distrust written all over his face. He looks at the photo and back at me. He enters the record and types the number into his computer to check for its authenticity and my past history, although I don't have much of a history with driving. He then cross-checks my details before tossing the licence in our direction.

'Who are you of her?' he points at me and Cecelia. He wants to know our relationship.

'I'm her aunt,' Cecelia says in her Canadian accent. 'We live in a joint family.'

His eyes scan her attire. 'You don't look related.'

'Yeah, well her uncle married me when we were in…'

'Okay okay,' he says, not quite interested in hearing the whole story. Then his eyes shift to us. 'This boy was kissing her.' He makes a face that screams disgust. 'This is today's generation. Late at night, they don't have any shame.'

I start to say something, anger gnawing at my chest, but Cecelia speaks up. 'Officer, you said she was wearing a helmet, driving at an acceptable speed, in a straight line without holding up traffic and wasn't breaking any specific rule other than this. Now you have all the documents and penalty fees, too. Right?'

The cop narrows his eyes at her, and nods slowly.

'So kindly stop moral policing,' she says, her tone is polite but nothing like the soft-spoken one laced with sweetness and awe that I'm used to. It is curt and means business. If I didn't know her personally, I'd be wearing the exact same expression the cop has on his face. He's gritting his teeth, but evidently holding his tongue.

'Jaise bade, waise chote.' (Like old, like young) He thumps his file on the desk and shakes his head before dismissing us. Cecelia doesn't bother to ask me to translate his last sentence. She looks done with everything.

The minute we're out and far out of sight from the police station, she turns to me. 'I want you home,' she says. I've never imagined her being capable of ordering anyone around. The image of her in my mind is taking a different shape.

'And you,' she whips around to look at Darshak, who suddenly stands straight like a soldier and I snort, without meaning to. 'Is this a laughing matter to you?' She gives me a sharp look and I shake my head, my smile dying on my face.

'I want both of you home in half an hour. I'll be in a taxi behind you. And I'll make sure you drop her home. Once I'm convinced you're both in your respective homes and not sneaking out somewhere else, I'll go back to office.'

Neither of us opposes her. We wait for her to get into a cab and then Darshak and I ride silently all the way home. Darshak drops me and shakes my hand awkwardly, both of us aware that Cecelia is in the cab behind us.

'Drive safe. Text me when you reach home.'

'I'm sorry...' he starts and I shake my head.

'Please, not now. Let's keep this conversation for some other day.'

He nods, equally exhausted by the day.

'See you tomorrow?'

I hear a throat clearing beside us and I know Cecelia is standing two feet away from us now, her hands crossed over her chest, waiting for Darshak to get going.

He smiles sadly at her, mounts his bike and zooms out of sight. I turn to Cecelia, hanging my head. She doesn't say a word, but I can feel her stare.

'Thank you,' I mutter. Then something happens that I don't expect. I don't realize I do it, until I find myself in her arms. I literally throw myself at Cecelia and before I know it, I'm sobbing in her arms.

She is taken aback as well. But she relaxes into the hug and pats the top of my head. 'It's okay.'

I shake my head. 'No it's not. I'm so, so, so sorry for what I did. What I said to you. I know I don't deserve an ounce of your good nature. What you just did, it just…'

'Hey, it's okay,' she says and holds me at arm's length. 'It really is. Just make sure next time you choose a less busy day to get into trouble,' she adds and I smile through my tears.

'I'll make it up to you,' I reply and mean it.

'Okay. And now, I should go.'

I nod and we both insist on waiting till the other is safely out of sight. But then she has the last word and I run to my balcony just in time to see her cab disappear around the corner.

Chapter Nineteen

The next morning, I'm up before dawn. I take a bath, get ready and rummage through the kitchen to find what I need. There is a little salad, two packets of penne pasta, cheese, some mayonnaise (enough for one-time use) and that's it. I make a list of things I'll need and jog down my lane. I scurry around buying bread, pasta and pizza sauce, cucumbers, tomatoes, beetroot, all of which are as fresh as they can get and run back home. There's still an hour or so before 9:30 or 10:00, which is when Cecelia and Dad will be home.

I prepare the basic two-layer sandwiches and sauté onions, garlic, chilli flakes and boiled pasta in one pan when I hear the door knob turn, followed by noises.

'Is she still asleep?'

'Guess so.'

'Do you smell something funny?' this is Cecelia. I wait for Dad to reply. When he doesn't, I look over my shoulder.

'You're awake?' Dad's at the door, his expression a mixture of surprise and disbelief. 'Or am I so sleepy, I'm starting to imagine things?'

I giggle. 'Welcome home, Papa.'

'Wow,' Cecelia says while she examines the table I've set with knives and forks. As I add grated cheese and ready-made Italian sauce to the blend, she stops near me and inches closer to smell the pasta that's almost ready. 'Mmm,' she drawls.

Dad runs his hand over my head like he can't believe I'm behaving like a grown-up. 'Your mother would be so proud.'

I roll my eyes and shrug his hand off. 'Dad, stop embarrassing me. You sound like I never cook anything.'

'That's because you don't,' he says matter-of-factly. Well, I don't argue with that, but he need not mention it.

'Whatever.'

Cecelia looks exactly like she did last night, with the top button of her shirt loose, blazer in her hand. The corners of their eyes are red and I can see tiredness on their faces.

'Freshen up. I'll finish up and serve by then.'

'Thank you, *beta*,' Dad says, looking a bit too proud and pleased. I don't like that look, so I push him towards the kitchen entrance.

'Go.'

About half an hour later, we're at the table munching on breakfast. I'm especially pleased to see the two of them gobbling the food silently. It's obvious they're hungry beyond words and even though this is a little thank you gift to Cecelia, I feel glad I decided to prepare a filling meal. Dad needs a break too.

'I don't know if they will approve of the whole thing we built yesterday,' Cecelia says when we're almost done eating.

'Never think about the results. Give it your best shot,' Dad says and chews the last bite of his sandwich. 'But I'm positive. That entire model cost us a lot more than what they hoped we'd build for them. Plus, it'll be done in two more days. And we're almost ready with the presentation. No chance to feel diffident.'

Cecelia nods and reaches for her glass of water. When she is done drinking it, she picks up her plate to bring it to the sink and suddenly stops. She squints at a tiny note on the table under her plate. Dad doesn't notice when a smile touches her lips and a look of forgiveness passes between the two of us. On her way to the sink, she rests her hand on my head and gives it a gentle nod, as if to say, *yes*.

The note read: *Friends?*

* * *

That afternoon in college, I bunk lectures and help with my share of the volunteering work that's been piling up. I haven't been to college for four days, including Saturday and Sunday. If you're a part of a fest, there are no non-working days.

Generally, my work includes helping to make posters, tacking them up on walls, talking to teachers about games unique to each department, running errands to gather items, putting up stalls, sitting at protocol desks for hours waiting for students to show up, taking down names of participants and collecting their money, co-ordinating with Divya, the anchor of the show and her work and just volunteering around.

As soon as I'm done with whatever my seniors bark at me to do, I flee to watch Darshak's rehearsals. I haven't been there to cheer him and his band on for almost a week now. I have no idea how the songs have progressed. They are going to perform on stage for an hour both days of the function. They have meticulously selected different types of songs. There is something for everyone: soft Hindi and English melodies, remixes and some popular film songs.

During rehearsals, Fatima, the dancer of our group, and I sit on the side benches ready to applaud when the band hits the right notes. After about an hour of watching them practise (which is boring when all you have to do is sit there and watch them tune their instruments or sing songs in broken patches), I turn to her. She is reading her dance notes and making some weird gestures with her hands, probably silently practising the moves.

'Don't you have your dance rehearsals?' I ask her.

'I do. In about an hour,' she says without stopping whatever classical movements and expression she's making. If you didn't know she was practising, you might have thought she was unstable. 'But we are almost done with our performance. I worry more about the Racketeers than my group.'

I search my mind to pin point the familiar name. The Racketeers. 'Is that Shreya's dance group?'

'Yah.'

'Why? What happened?'

She shrugs. 'One of their dance members left their group and joined mine saying dancing with the Racketeers was a waste of her time and talent.'

I raise a brow. 'That's a strong statement to make.'

'And true. They are planning to perform a couple's dance, but their tutor said she can't teach them anymore.'

'Why?'

She shrugs. 'Some personal reasons. What we suspect is that she hated teaching them.'

I have seen Shreya and her group dance a couple of times in the recreation-cum-dance room. But more than practising, I have seen her argue with her group. They are probably the least favourite of the teachers. They hardly have any unity. I reckon the girl who left them isn't at fault here. I mean, I wouldn't blame her for ditching them.

'I thought they performed Bollywood every year,' I say remembering their previous performances.

'Yes, but they wanted to experiment this time around.' She rolls her eyes and flips a page of her book. 'First they should learn to work together and then probably try and experiment. They argue about every little thing. From which songs to choose to who will stand where. Nobody is pleased with anyone else's suggestion. They will be rejected this time, *pakka*.'

I scoff. *How did they manage to even stick around for so many years*, I wonder.

Chapter Twenty

Fatima leaves for her dance practice an hour later. Nothing more productive to do, I add all the boys back into our WhatsApp group chat from Purti's phone and apologize on our behalf. It is fun to have healthy fights now and then, but frustrating if we stretch them. When Darshak's phone vibrates in his pocket, he pulls it out and smiles. He types back a reply. 'Apology accepted, lovely ladies.' He sends the message.

After about an hour, a girl knocks on our door and pokes her head in. Sudden silence descends over the room like a class going silent when a teacher walks in.

We fiercely protect our privacy. The last thing we want is an outsider witnessing our half-baked performance.

'Neha Ranade?' she looks around the hall, her eyes resting on every face for a second. When I raise my hand, she says, 'Tanna Ma'am wants to see you.'

Tanna Ma'am is the chief organizer of our entire two-day annual function. She is the one who sends students to numerous colleges and invites those students to ours. She brings in big sponsors and looks after the finances.

She is also the vice-principal of our college. She informs our seniors of the tasks, who in turn charge at us. We then do the donkey work, trying to get shit together.

Though I'm not in direct touch with her, I've heard enough stories to form a stern picture of her in my mind. She refuses to take no for an answer and holds grudges against those who cross her.

It isn't a pretty picture.

I do not plan to go down on her list. I still have two years, so I do not want to exist as another walking dead student in the college struggling to survive. I want to live and explore everything I can. So I follow the girl and knock on the door that reads Richa S. Tanna before pushing it open.

'Neha Ranade,' I say and wait at the entrance.

Tanna Ma'am, who is leafing through a newspaper, looks up and her eyes go warm with a smile when she sees me. Her smile is a rare occurrence. And directing it to one of her students? That'd be a dream.

Or perhaps a nightmare.

'Take a seat,' she says.

I thank her, pull out a cushioned chair and take a seat as quietly as I can, not wanting to disrupt the uncomfortable silence.

This is the first time I've entered her cabin. I see the middle of our college quad through the wide window behind her. Guys play football, NSS committee kids march on the ground, some wait in line near office windows. Images of us goofing around in that quad, pulling and hitting each other, clicking tons of duck-faced selfies, hugging, and Darshak and I getting cozy pop into my mind. I decide I'll be more disciplined the next time I enter that area. You never know when you'll be under the microscope.

'You wanted to see me, Ma'am?' I ask, waiting for her to bark orders.

'Yes. How are you doing today?' She scans my face over her thick glasses. Her cabin is brightly lit. A light above her head makes her skin glow and her nails shine. Her usual authoritative and strict face appears laidback. That is when I realize I'm not in trouble. Besides, I'm not someone important for her to be bothered with.

The tension in my shoulders relaxes. 'I'm fine, Ma'am. Thank you.'

'Good.'

I stroke my left hand over my bare arm without giving much thought to it.

'Feeling cold?' she asks.

'No, Ma'am,' I lie and a gust of cold air from the AC makes me shudder. 'I'm fi—'

But before I can complete the sentence, she hits a button on a remote control and the AC and room go silent. I raise a brow. Why am I being treated so preciously? An image of a well-fed chicken about to be butchered pops in my mind.

She places her glasses on the newspaper. 'So Neha, how was yesterday's show?'

I blink. 'Sh… Show?'

'Yeah. At Prithvi Theatre?'

How does she know about it? Was she there, too? 'It was… it was good.'

'I guessed so.' She slides *The Café* newspaper in my direction, page four on top. I peer at it. It takes me a moment to realize what I'm looking at. When I do, I feel blood rush to my face.

I'm looking back at my own pictures. Cecelia, Darshak and I are standing next to Genelia Deshmukh and Rachael Biswas, a famous theatre actress who played the parallel lead of the mother in the play. She is a beautiful woman only a few years older than Cecelia. Apparently, this play is supposed to be her big comeback. She asked us how we liked the show last night and I remember blabbering on about how much I loved it. Cecelia is shaking hands with her in that picture.

A caption under that photo reads: *The return of theatre queen, Rachael Biswas, pictured here with some fans.*

Under another picture, it reads: *Genelia and Riteish bonding with overseas art lovers.* In this one, Cecelia and the Deshmukhs are sitting in Prithvi Cafe with us, while a few people surround us. That must have been when the mob rushed in and called for their chief guests.

I am clutching Cecelia's elbow in the third picture. My eyes are huge with awe and I'm beaming. Darshak's arms are crossed beside me, a strained expression on his face. We both look out of place. The pictures are candid. I especially look star stuck and Darshak seems lost.

That was exactly how we felt. I decide that I'm going to frame these pictures first thing when I walk out of here. I look at Ma'am when I come out of the daze.

'Do you think you could contact Genelia and her husband and ask them to be our guests at the annual function?'

I stare at her.

'Don't talk about fees and all. Leave that to me. You just give them my number and ask them to call me whenever they're free. I'll do the rest of the talking.'

'I—'

'It would be good for our college's reputation, you know. And going by the pictures, you and your aunt seem to know them quite well.'

'How do you—'

'Darshak told me she was your aunt and that you're well acquainted with them. You even exchanged numbers.' Her eyes shine.

Change in plans. The first thing I'll do when I walk out of here is strangle Darshak. He knows we bumped into the stars by accident and they were just being kind and friendly. It isn't as if our existence really matters to them.

Besides, we exchanged e-mail ids, not phone numbers.

'There's no hurry. You can go home, talk to your aunt and then tell me. We'd be honoured to have them here, wouldn't we?'

'I'll do whatever I can, Ma'am.' I press my lips into a thin line, which is meant to be a smile and rise. In the same dazed state, I thank her once again—I have no clue why, probably for noticing me after three years—and leave quietly.

I wanted to refuse, but I couldn't. I couldn't possibly disappoint the only teacher students go into a frenzy to impress. I'm definitely in trouble.

Chapter Twenty-One

I go home, shoulders stooped with defeat. When Cecelia opens the door to me, I hand my bag to her and set off to my bedroom without glancing back. I wave at Rocky to let him know I've heard him, but he'll have to wait for a cuddle.

Cecelia tosses my bag into the living room and follows me. She starts to say something, probably telling me about the photo in the newspaper, but I shut the room door in her face. I regret it the minute I do.

At the dining table that night, I apologize and she stares at me like she can read my mind. 'Tell me what's upsetting you and I might forgive you.'

'What happened?' Dad slurps *dal*, glancing at me over his bowl. 'All fine?'

I avoid eye contact. I can feel both pairs of eyes studying me.

I *know* Cecelia can't help me. She met the couple at the theatre for the first time herself. Besides, I hadn't really treated her well since she arrived here. Why would she want to reach out to me now?

My phone vibrates in my loose pyjama pocket. I jerk and invite weird glances. Thankfully, with one look at me and then at each other, they let it pass. Just when I settle back into my chair to enjoy the last piece of *roti*, my pocket vibrates as if an earthquake has hit it. Continuous WhatsApp messages pour in.

I stuff the bite of food in my mouth, pick my plate up, dump it into the sink, run the tap water on high over my hands and rush to the living room. When I swipe my phone open, I scroll down to a hundred frenzied messages all fuming over Darshak and me. Purti is apparently sitting on a hot stove and texting. She sends in red-faced emoticons like she owns them.

They've seen our picture in the newspaper and it's quite the talk of the town. Since we were supposed to stick together against the guys, the girls especially have a fit about my being partial to Darshak.

I spend about fifteen minutes explaining that it was just a show and that they are overreacting, which angers them further. I close the chat in defeat. Cecelia strolls out with a box of white chocolates. She offers me one, sitting on the sofa next to me.

'I'm still waiting,' she says. I pop a chocolate in my mouth and let my taste buds dance to the sweetness.

'I need your help.'

She waits. Summoning up some courage, I narrate everything to her. The picture in the newspaper, the assumptions our teacher made, her expectations. I tell her I know it's all ridiculous. We happened to meet the stars out of sheer luck and they were just being friendly. We shouldn't take advantage of it. And anyway, I doubt Genelia would be able to reply on time, even if we decide to drop her a mail.

At the end, I emphasize that if Cecelia doesn't want to,

I'll tell Tanna Ma'am she got the wrong end of the stick and misunderstood the photos. And that we're sorry, we can't help her. I also fake a laugh at the end to make it all seem like it isn't a big deal.

'Are we done?' she asks at the end. I open my mouth and close it a few times. It seems like she can see through me for what she says next makes me want to jump at her and give her a bear hug.

'I'll e-mail her asking if she can make it. We'll wait for two days. If she doesn't get back to us, I'll see if I can reach Rachael Biswas or Riteish Deshmukh.' I ask if it is really possible. 'There's nothing wrong with trying. And we'd be paying for her visit, wouldn't we? So there's nothing to be ashamed of.' She shrugs, talking as if she belongs to our college, what with using 'we' and all.

I pull out my laptop. After about a dozen edits, we send them a letter, just the right mix between formal and informal. Frankly, I don't even care if the reply is positive or negative as long as I have an answer and proof to go along with it to show that I tried.

At night, I clutch Cecelia by the arm and spin us both around. The reply mail reads:

Cecelia Barnes,

I'm Divya Ahuja, Genelia Deshmukh's publicist. I read through your mail and had a word with Gen. She is busy for the next few months and won't have time for anything but shoots and ad campaigns. She regrets deeply having to turn you down.

However, I'm pleased to inform you that she contacted Rachael Biswas immediately after. I hope you're acquainted with her. She asked if Rachael could attend your function on her behalf.

And I'm glad to say Mrs Biswas is ready. Plus, if it suits you, she'd perform a skit or an excerpt from her new play at your function with her team.

You can get in touch with her directly via her number or mail ID.

Best regards,

Divya Ahuja

* * *

I print the mail and present it to Tanna Ma'am the next day. And to my relief, she seems as eager to have Rachael Biswas as our guest as she was to have Genelia.

This whole thing promotes me onto her favourites list. She starts asking me to handle all the important tasks, like getting cheques from our sponsors or holding auditions for replacement dancers, anchors and musicians, much to my seniors' contempt. Not that I have a problem with it. Now I have more work offstage than I ever did before.

Chapter Twenty-Two

That evening, my friends and I wait under the blazing sun outside college near the Tibbs stall. We'd ordered seven *paneer* schezwaan frankies.

'I'm broke,' I say.

'So am I.' Purti raises her hand to escape paying.

'So am I,' two more voices echo. The last person to put his hand up is Darshak as he taps the keypad of his phone with urgent, flying fingers. He looks angry and oblivious to our lame 'you pay' game. I pull out my wallet when the frankies are passed on and pay on his behalf.

'What's the matter, baby?' I say after an hour as we walk towards the long bus queue. I peep at his phone and see a guy's name at the top of his WhatsApp chat. There are long angry messages and red devil emojis throughout the chat. I'm relieved to find out it isn't his ex.

But the relief is short-lived. I have to know what he is up to. So while his nose is glued to his phone, I casually loop my arm through his. Maybe the gentle touch would snuff out some flames. 'I've been watching you since morning. You look kinda upset.'

He doesn't respond. I withdraw my hand and bump my shoulder into him. He doesn't budge an inch, so I bump again and when he glances down, I wriggle my brows. He snorts. 'Don't make me laugh.'

'I love you when you laugh.'

'And when I don't?'

I shrug. 'I feel like making you laugh.'

He smiles.

'What's the matter? What's the matter? What's the matter?' I sing, getting loud enough for people walking by to shoot us weird looks.

'What are you doing, Neha?'

'Trying to bring a smile to those luscious lips.'

The top of his lip twitches. That means my favourite kind of smirk and some sarcastic remark is on the way. 'Try harder.' He smirks like I had predicted. 'I've taught you better than that.'

My mouth goes wide enough for a *pani puri* to slide in. 'Okay,' I say and tickle him right under the ribcage. He grabs my wrists and holds me at arm's length.

'Spare me!' After about fifteen minutes of my endless *masti*, he spills the beans. 'I cancelled the trek.'

'What?' I stare at him. 'Why?'

'You're not there on that day,' he says, now ignoring the messages on his phone and switching it off. 'Was that so hard to figure out?'

Of all the things, I hadn't expected this to be his answer. Not from a guy who always finds a way around sticky situations and who is mostly relaxed under stress, which is a necessity when you have to deal with a crowd of hundreds when you're on stage, sometimes even when they are booing you.

He stops suddenly before crossing the road, pushing his arm out in front of me. I skid to a halt behind him. 'Gosh! Watch out.' His voice is irritated. A car zooms so close past us, my hair dances in the sudden gust of wind.

'You don't need to do that Darshak,' I say, sensing he's still pissed off from the phone conversation. 'You guys go, please.'

'I don't want to. Besides, it's not just you. There're only seven people in the trek group. They need fifteen at the least.'

'Who else dropped out?'

'Five of you,' he says. 'Even out of the four of us who're still going, only Purti and I seem excited about it.'

'That's not true. You can arrange a private trek later with us. But this time—'

'I said I don't want to,' he cuts in. Trekking is the lifeline of our group. We'd known one another since junior college, but we had actually bonded on the first trek we had gone on.

One morning on a boring practice day, Darshak had timidly put forth the idea of going on a trek. That was back when we politely listened to each other's advice and kept quiet when someone spoke. As opposed to flinging sticks and throwing our hands up in frustration, interrupting statements and discarding ideas two years down the line.

So when Darshak had asked, we had quietly contemplated it for a few minutes. And needless to say, I had been the first one to raise my hand and announce I was in. You can't blame me for being too eager. I had been suffering from love-at-first-sight syndrome.

And when we all returned from this excursion, tired and worn out but with ear-to-ear grins across our faces, we knew this bond had just become ten times stronger. Since then, we made it a point to go on a trek every three months. Darshak was an old member of Trek Stars, an established trek group that frequently organized short hikes. He was also on the deciding committee.

He also arranged and initiated treks just for the eight of us when we wished to go, but there were no immediate TS treks lined up. I have always been an avid trekker and I was surprised and delighted to learn Darshak loved it too.

'I just need to break this news to the rest,' Darshak says and his temple looks like its throbbing. It throbs whenever he feels particularly angry or helpless.

'I don't think they'll take it well.' I remember how Hiten was trashed for days for ditching. I haven't told them I'm not planning to come as well. And Darshak has definitely not told them he has chucked the whole thing altogether. The larger the group, the more the drama, the more the opinions and the more the tantrums.

'Can you save this one trek?' I ask after we shove our way through the bus crowd, Darshak sticking close behind me.

'I already cancelled it, Neha,' he says. 'I fought with sir to postpone it. But when he refused, I said we would all back out. Now let's see how the hell they go.' If we cancel, it would drop the number of hikers by three quarters. And if that happens, all the bookings, money and planning would kiss the dust.

'What if I come?'

He casts a sideway glance at me. 'As if.'

'No, I'm serious.' Suddenly, I feel this problem isn't unsolvable at all. 'Tell me, will you?'

'Maybe. Can you?' His voice is a little less strained now and I see colour rush to his face.

'Yes.' The corner of my lips curve. 'As long as you allow Cecelia to tag along.'

Chapter Twenty-Three

With all the work dumped on me, I can't give Cecelia the time and entertainment she deserves, so instead, I take her out for shopping. With my ulterior motives that she is well aware of, she pampers me thoroughly.

Instead of hovering around college for too long, I skip band practices and everything else that requires my passive presence, race home by four and take her out shopping for the next five days.

We shop and explore places Mumbai's famous for: Hill Road, Linking Road, Colaba Causeway. From popular street shopping spots to malls like High Street Phoenix or R-city, I take her on an elaborate Mumbai tour. We go to the Gateway of India and the Worli Sea Link on Saturday. Being an art lover, she takes hours to stroll through Jehangir Gallery which bores me to tears, but I let her explore at her pace.

When we return, Cecelia knocks on my room door asking for sunburn lotion. When I insist she show me her burns, ignoring her, 'It's nothing, I'm fine,' I almost flip.

The skin around her collarbones, neck and arms is red. A few blisters have appeared on her back. Her face has reddened, but isn't affected as much as her upper body is.

I stuff handkerchiefs with loads of ice and rest them on the parts that are burned. I switch the AC on in her room and direct the blower towards her while applying aloe vera gel on her back and leaving a mixture of turmeric and water on her blisters. While I'm doing that, she says, lying on her stomach, 'It's okay, Nayha. I'm fine. It isn't the first time the sun's kissed me.'

'Shhh.' I hand her the cold lemon sherbet and watch her sip it slowly, almost against her will. 'Act like a guest and lie down quietly.'

She smiles, but does as she's told.

* * *

The next day, Sunday, Dad is home and Cecelia's skin is just starting to recover. So we spend the day at home, playing cards, Scrabble, listening to music and sharing stories. In the evening, when I'm rubbing cream on her bare back, Dad walks in on us.

'Oh sorry,' he says, turning around quickly.

'Dad!' I whisper under my breath. 'Get out.' I hear Cecelia laugh softly under the towel.

'I'm sorry. I just wanted to ask what you want for dinner.'

'Ordering?' I ask.

'No. Cooking.'

I try to think of my favourite dish, one that is not too spicy, but still richly flavoured. That is when Cecelia speaks up, 'How about this?' She turns around, hugging the towel to her chest. 'Today I'll cook. Poutine, baked chicken and spinach flautas and pizza. We'll buy ice-cream and have an elaborate three-course meal with wine.'

Dad and I are quiet for some time. 'Sounds... fancy,' I

say, not sure if I've heard half the names.

'And I'm sure Mr. Ranade won't mind. He's spent all those years eating only our food. It will refresh his memory.'

Dad thinks about it. 'Okay,' he says, his back still to us. 'As long as you don't burn down my kitchen.'

'We won't.' She smiles and turns to me. 'You'll help me?'

I nod, already excited to find out what those dishes are, since Dad, being the secretive, silent person that he is, never mentioned eating them.

* * *

We step into the Phoenix Mall at Lower Parel two days later when Cecelia has fully recovered and shop till our arms can carry no more. As we browse through lip glosses at the MAC counter, my phone buzzes. Cursing the caller for interrupting us, I swipe the red button and pat my lips. The phone buzzes again after a few seconds.

'Take it.' Cecelia looks at me. I examine the red gloss in the mirror, feeling her gaze on me. I sigh, pull out my phone and swipe the green dot.

'Helloo?' I elongate the 'O' to check how my painted lips look when I curl them. They look sexy.

A barrage of questions blasts out of the other end and I hold the phone away from my ear. 'Where are you? When are you coming back? Is Cecelia with you too?'

Cecelia gestures at me asking who it is. I roll my eyes and, with my left hand, mime someone talking on and on. Someone on the other end is talking endlessly. She smiles, turns to the girl waiting on us and asks her the price of the gloss I'm wearing.

'Yah. Bye. Love you too,' I say and dump the phone in my bag. When we walk out of the store with my Russian Red gloss, and out of the mall, we hail a cab and head to Bandra Bandstand. The cab driver honks his way through a crowd of people crossing the road at random. Cecelia clutches my hand for dear life.

'We'll kill pedestrians if we keep up this speed,' she squeaks, gasping every time someone walks too closely to the cars. I laugh. While we make our way to our destination, she asks me a little later, 'Where are we headed?'

'Bandstand,' I tell her. 'It's a place where people go to see Mannat first and then the beach.'

'What's may-not?' Cecelia asks, amused.

'Not may-not. Mannat. M-A-N-N-A-T.' I spell it out. 'It's where India's biggest superstar lives—Shah Rukh Khan.'

'Oh that guy!' She's apparently heard a few things about him. For one, she knows he's treated like a god in India, is called 'the King of Bollywood' and is one of the richest celebs in the world. She has also seen one of his movies, one she can't recall the name of. So she knows him enough to get all bouncy when I declare we'll go see him… or rather his house.

We look at the waves, splashy Bandstand waters and eat corn and the Indian burger or *wada pav*. She loves the spicy taste of it in her mouth, though she has to sip cold water after every bite. She orders it herself in her broken Hindi and loves the frothy cutting *chai*.

'*Bhaiyya, eik cutting chaye day na,*' she says. My phone vibrates again.

'We are coming home in an hour. Quit calling!' I snap

and hang up the phone to distant protests. Cecelia stares at me with a pointed, disapproving look. I squirm under it.

'I know that was rude and I shouldn't have lied.' It'd take us a lot more than an hour to reach home. 'But it's a white lie.' I shrug sheepishly, trying to defend my tone during the call. 'And if we're late, which we will be, it'll just make it clear we are having a great time.'

She shakes her head and I wait for a lecture, but it doesn't come. Instead, she turns to pay for our food without a word. Her silence is deafening. Somehow, the fact that she doesn't say anything makes me feel guiltier. I make a mental note to apologize to Dad.

After approximately four hours and twenty-five minutes, we climb the steps to our apartment and ring the doorbell. My dad flings it open. He takes one look at me and starts bombarding me with questions.

'You won't pick up my calls. You sound all irritated when you do pick up. You say you'll be back in an hour and then take an eternity to come home! Girl, you will give your father a heart attack one day.'

I stand on my tip toes, kiss his cheek and walk past him. 'Sorry for being like that. But don't you ever get tired of asking questions?'

Cecelia follows me inside. I see her mouth 'sorry' to him on her way in.

Massive shopping bags hang from our shoulders. Our smiles, good spirits and hefty bags are proof enough that we had a good time. When we finally sit down, my dad repeats his questions. This time though I decide to put an end to his concern.

'Papa, relax. First, I'm sorry. It was all my idea.'

He frowns, looking like an angry kid who's been refused an extra cookie. 'That I guessed. And the fact that Cecelia didn't pick up her phone proved you two were in it together.'

'The last couple of days we figured we've got to have some fun. She is in India for the first time and she ought to get to know the city better.'

He looks surprised. 'Is that so?'

I ignore the cynicism in his tone. 'So as soon as I came home after college, we went to different places around the city. Visited authentic Indian restaurants, beaches, went street shopping. Stuff like that.' Cecelia nods while unpacking the box of cupcakes. 'And since you were in office all day, we figured it wouldn't be necessary to inform you. You wanted me to show her around, anyway, didn't you?'

'But you could have told me that over the phone. I get half a day off and come home to find you both gone, vanished. No one picking up my calls, no notes, no messages.'

'It's more fun to go on expeditions without telling anyone,' I smile. 'You should try it too.'

'Yeah, right. And get kicked out of office.' He snorts, eyeing the box of cupcakes.

'You didn't think we would get lost or that I would abduct Cecelia, did you?' I watch Cecelia tear the box open and offer him one.

'Of course not.' Dad picks a red velvet cupcake with vanilla icing and takes a generous bite, the scowl on his forehead relaxing when the taste hits him. 'But then I come home early and find the two of you gone, nowhere to be seen. It scares your old man.' He locks his gaze on Cecelia. 'And I didn't believe you could be in on it.'

'Surprise,' she mouths. She and I air high five each other.

'Your surprise had me waiting outside for an hour. Who told you to carry the house keys with you?' His tone softens when he takes another bite of the cupcake. 'I had to go all the way to your aunt's house and get the spare ones.'

'Now chuck it, Daddy,' I say. 'We said we're sorry.' I wave my hand behind his back, gesturing at her to indicate that we aren't. Cecelia and I chuckle.

'You will make my colleague crazy along with you,' he says, shaking his head and I cross my heart.

Chapter Twenty-Four

I never expected I'd like Cecelia so much. She is modern, open minded, helpful and extremely caring.

The night before we are to go to Adlabs Imagica, I wrinkle my nose at my reflection in the mirror. I'm wearing shorts that reveal my naturally wheatish legs. But contrary to it, my face and hands have succumbed to the cruel weather. They have tanned to a point where no amount of face or body wash can scrub it off. My hair sticks out in all directions and I have a huge zit sprouting out of one of my cheeks.

Pathetic!

While packing food for our trip early in the morning, I ask Cecelia, 'Why can't we just have the best hair and skin days every day?'

'Does it really matter?'

'OF COURSE.' I look at her as if she's sprouted horns. 'Who doesn't want to look good every day? I know I do.'

'You look fine.' She presses a slice of cheese down over her salad. She's made a three-tier tower, each layer yummier than the one below. 'You look younger today than you ever will in all your life.'

I gape at her for a moment before picking up the sandwich she had made and setting it neatly in a box. 'That didn't make me feel any better.'

She giggles, dropping four slices of bread into the toaster, and pulls out a chair to sit on. 'Let me let you in on a secret. When you're old, you'll look back and realize you looked just fine, in fact, better than fine.' She looks at me as I suppress my temptation to taste those monstrous grilled sandwiches.

'You'll understand the value of your teenage years when you're not a teenager anymore. Don't waste this time thinking about what you lack, especially with regard to your looks. With age, all that'll stay with you is your heart and your brain, which translates into character and knowledge. One will define the relationships in your life and the other will define your career. That is all that will matter in the long run. Plus, you're always slightly more beautiful than you think you are.'

I blink at her. 'You think so?'

'I know so. The more you stare at something, the more you start to see the flaws in it. The same goes for your face. Beauty is very short-lived and overrated. None of those supposed 'cool' things—marks, looks, being popular, having the coolest kids call you a friend—matter a flying frog when you're on your own.'

I stare at her for more time than I should. She asks me what I am thinking. I shake my head, wondering if my mom would have explained the same things the same way had she been alive.

When it's time finally to go to Adlabs Imagica, I load my rucksack with newly bought clothes and accessories. I don't regret having to spend two full days with Cecelia. In fact, I'm kind of looking forward to it.

When we reach the theme park, we explore Aquamagica for a day and return to our hotel room, exhausted and a little more tanned.

Cecelia is off to get some Ayurvedic massage that screamed 'special discount' on the pamphlet. I sprawl on the double bed in the cozy room, browsing through song lists and pictures on my laptop, my legs swinging and my mouth munching on hot finger chips.

I'd have called Darshak to talk to him about how I conquered my fear and attempted a scary water ride with a free vertical drop from forty feet up, but he is busy playing football. Football is his second love. Keeps him fit and energized, he says. He loves playing whenever he has the time. And from what I see of him during his local tournaments, he looks quite hot running around in shorts and sweaty t-shirts.

But being the lead vocalist of his band and the band being quite in demand, most of his time is either spent in rehearsals or *riyaaz*. The rest of the time... well, he has a girlfriend, so he ought to give her some time too.

I don't demand it, though, especially when I know he would be busy. So instead of pestering him with calls, I let him be while I play our favourite song, so I'll miss him less. When I come across *Million Reasons Why*, I spring up on the bed and sit on my heels.

It's been ages since I last heard this song. As a huge fan of the Game Players, the night I learnt they had come out with a new single, I downloaded it before I had listened to it. I had pushed one of my earphone buds into Darshak's ear on our bus ride home and had scrolled through lyrics on my phone for him to see.

By the end of our ride, Darshak had snatched the bud in my ear and had hit repeat thrice. When we hopped off the bus, he had transferred the song to his phone and on my birthday a month later, played an acoustic version of it when we were alone in the music room. Then, we had shared one of our most passionate kisses right there, and we pulled away just in time to hear a shift of feet outside the room.

Those days…

So this is *our song*. Now that I couldn't reach him, I let it play on my speakers, while I croon as loudly as I can to it.

I crawl up on the bed after the first stanza. I roll up the menu card lying beside the table and double it up as a mic. I tap my feet, pretending to charm a crowd of hundreds.

When the song hits the chorus, I hear a voice humming to the song. I stop in my tracks. The voice, which is slightly more in tune, isn't mine. The knob turns and a figure in shorts emerges from behind the single bedroom door. Cecelia walks in, presses the function key on my laptop and raises the volume.

'You know this song?' I ask over the blasting speakers, my eyes wide. She smiles without stopping, sways her hips in perfect circles and gestures for me to join her in. But I only stare. I don't join in partly because I am too self-conscious to open my mouth and sing and partly because the way she moves is mesmerizing. The grace and finesse of her moves make me want to keep looking at her.

When the song hits the bridge, she twirls on one leg and without putting that foot down, she leans forward towards me, her movements slow and graceful. She brings her face close to mine and plants a kiss on my cheek, all that to the beats of the song. Then she straightens, with her leg still in the air. She puts her feet on the ground with a twirl and takes an elaborate bow.

When the song ends she slumps down on the bed, making it bounce a couple of times and glances up at me.

I'm lost. I touch my cheek where she kissed me. 'That is probably the best kiss of my life,' I say in a daze and she laughs. Her fingers linger over the touchpad, politely pausing before asking my permission to restart the song. Manners. I roll my eyes and she hits play.

I jump down on the ground. 'Can you teach me what you just did?'

To hell with the song being secret and personal. I desperately want to groove like her.

She takes my hand without a word and spins me around twice, so forcefully I stumble into her. She takes a step back so I won't bump and cause her to lose her balance. I learn early on that if I want her to teach me, I have to be prepared to sweat.

The next time she spins me, I twist after two quick swings and balance on my tip toes.

Chapter Twenty-Five

The second day of our trip especially paces my heart beats. Cecelia and I go for almost all the family rides and on my insistence, she tries one thrill ride, the Dare Drop, before deciding she wants to live a few more years. She says the ride rushed her blood to parts of her body she didn't know existed.

It gives her a headache that lasts a long time. I stay back with her, bringing her food and water, giving her a head massage, but she insists I make the most of our money. When I'm sure she's slightly better, I try everything that is too dangerous for her and we click loads of pictures on other rides.

We return home in the evening and both of us hit the sack. I don't realize when Dad is back, but I remember him taking turns waking us both quietly with music and the delicious aroma of ordered food.

With one short but deep nap, we're both awake and feeling better. After dinner, we rest for some time and Cecelia teaches me more of the dance. I practise that night till my stomach hurts.

* * *

I carry the euphoric feeling to college the next day. The reason is not just a trip to the theme park, but also learning basic Salsa steps to my favourite song. I'm so pumped up to show Darshak the dance that I pull him into the dance room first thing in the morning, making sure it is void of dancers, and push him into a seat.

'What? Am I getting a kiss or something?' He collapses, hindering his fall by holding the back of his chair. 'Or are you going to do a strip dance?' he pretends to close his eyes.

I'm too excited to explain. I lightly kick his feet, and he huffs in a very dramatic way. 'Relax on the violence,' he says. I pull out his phone and scroll down to find *Million Reasons Why*. I hit play when I find it.

I start off with stretching my arms over my head and standing on my toes. I spin around once and jump forward, swaying and twirling. I have no clue how clownish I look, but Darshak is the first person I want to show the dance to.

I glance at him in between my dance moves. He only stares at me with a weird expression on his face, like he is worried I'm possessed. But I'm enjoying this too much to care about his reaction. At the bridge of the song, I lean over to kiss Darshak on the cheek the same way Cecelia kissed me. My leg is up in the air and I'm standing on my tiptoes. His mouth drops open the minute I do this.

The song and my dance end with one of my arms out and a curtsy. I straighten, my chest rising and falling with deep breaths. I grin at him, eyes glinting, and wait to know what he thinks about it.

'What the eff?' Is all he manages to say from the seat I had dumped him on, in the same position as before, his hand holding the back of the chair and his legs crossed. The smile on my face dies. From his look, it seems he either isn't very happy or is so happy he forgot to react.

Shreya, a girl with a bouncy ponytail and wearing a

loose kurti, dashes into the room, her eyes wide. 'Where did you get those moves?'

I knew she was watching me from the door and I didn't mind. I was too in love with the dance to disrespect it and stop midway. In fact, I enjoyed the little audience.

'These moves. They are... signature!' she says. I had never seen her so excited before. 'These moves are professional moves. Where did you learn them? And how come you were able to do that spin cleanly?'

'Well, I—' I start, only to have her interrupt me.

'You took two quick spins on one leg without losing your balance. That's also a typical ballet pirouette!'

'Err, thanks,' I say, a little surprised at her enthusiasm.

'I've never seen you do this before,' Darshak says. 'Although you turn heads whenever you hit the floor on DJ nights and all. But you were mostly known for...'

'Ganpati dance?' I raise a brow at him and chuckle.

'Spontaneity,' he adds. 'Coming up with steps quick enough to match the song playing.'

I smile. 'Well, this wasn't spontaneous. Cecelia taught me this dance. She learnt a little bit of Salsa and some other dance forms back in Canada. She mixed the steps she learnt in her classes and choreographed this song when the Game Players were the talk of the town. I liked them and asked if she could teach me.'

'And when did you find time to learn all that?' Darshak gets to his feet, holding my gaze.

'At Imagica. I played this song in the hotel room when she appeared out of nowhere. She started to groove to it and

I knew I *had* to learn what she did. That feeling was so impulsive and intense, I skipped dinner and practised. It took me two full days though.'

'Two days. That's...' Shreya inaudibly murmurs something to herself. Shreya and Darshak exchange looks. 'Are you thinking what I'm thinking?' Shreya asks him, acting all Miss Jane Bond.

He shrugs. 'Probably. Since I know what you want.'

She beams at me. 'I'll be back. Please wait here.' She turns and dashes out of the room, dialling a number on the way. She looks like a girl on a mission.

I stare after her and crease my forehead. I point my thumb at her figure disappearing around the corner and ask, 'She's acting strange. What's wrong with her?'

Darshak blows air into his palms and looks at me like I'm a slice of fresh pizza and he's been starved for days.

I like that look.

'That was unexpected.'

'Oh-kay. That's creeping me out now,' I say, narrowing my eyes. 'What are you smiling about? And you didn't tell me if you liked the dance.'

He pulls a face. 'I think it was a mistake that you showed me your dance here.' He walks over to the music player and connects a long cord to his phone. 'We'll have to do this again.'

'Are you dancing with me now?' I stand beside him.

'No.' He adjusts a dial on the player and turns to face me. Pinching the tip of my nose, he bends in his knees, so we are the same height. I see my face reflected in his eyes. 'You are.'

Chapter Twenty-Six

'Whoa. Hold on. What?' I snap, wiping sweat off my brow. Darshak slips his hand into mine, without saying a word, as soon as I'm done dancing the second time. He gives my hand a gentle squeeze to convey he'd stick with me come what may.

After whooshing in and out like a whirlwind a few minutes ago, Shreya returned with the lead dancer of her group, Ritesh, and requested me to perform the same dance for him. 'He needs to see the steps, if you don't mind,' she had said.

I couldn't refuse point blank and risk appearing rude or arrogant. I assumed they wanted to steal a move or two and I was cool with it. If Ritesh liked it, which Shreya claimed he certainly would, they'd absorb it.

So I danced. And I was glad he not only liked the moves, but also the way *I* moved. But things did not end there.

Shreya is explaining now. 'We're not able to find a good dance teacher who can teach us western couples' dances. Finding a teacher for free is difficult, but finding a good one is next to impossible.

For the first time we want to dance to English mash-ups. But the unsettling part is the Racketeers will be rejected if we don't come up with something original and different.' Shreya tucks a tiny fringe behind her ear and it falls back against her brow. 'Your dance is almost exactly what we are looking for. I mean not *your* dance precisely, but the type of dance moves that you did. We are hoping to perform a piece much like that. Only in pairs.'

Ritesh sighs. 'Her point is that if the person who taught you these steps would help us out it would be a huge favour.'

They mean Cecelia. Talk about impossible demands.

I remember Fatima telling me this dance group, the Racketeers, was the weakest. One of their dancers ditched them to join Fatima and now no one is ready to be a part of their group.

I wouldn't mind helping if they asked me to teach them these steps or even replacing the girl who left them. But summoning the choreographer? Not so much.

Darshak stands still beside me. I want to shake him with the hope that a decision falls out of his mouth, but he only provides passive support.

'When do you have to perform for the selection?'

'In about two and a half weeks.'

'And you think that's enough?'

'More than.'

I sigh. Somehow two weeks seems too little time to me. I need, at the least, a year…

'You tricked me,' I mutter. Shreya smiles seeing that I've started to lay down my armour. 'I can't promise you anything. Frankly, I feel that you'd simply be rejected if I team up with him.' I point at Ritesh.

'Excuse me?' Ritesh squirms. He seems too uptight to bend. While Shreya pleaded with me, he stood there with an I-don't-care-about-this-anymore expression on his face.

Maybe he doesn't have much hope about getting selected either.

'No. I mean you're a great dancer. It's me I don't trust. I don't know if I could...'

'You're fine. Better than you know,' he says, dismissing my insecurity with a wave of his hand. It doesn't look like he means it.

'That's because Cecelia taught me every move. Besides, she only taught me the chorus, everything else was a variation or repetition. It was a short dance and it took me two full days to get it right.'

'Time doesn't matter,' he says like he is tired of this discussion. With the desperation with which Shreya rushed in and out of the room, I had assumed that they must have asked fifty dancers to fill in the vacancy and had been turned down by them all. Who knows?

'If you promise to help us, I promise I wouldn't let you go off beam. Even if we're on stage and you go blank,' Ritesh says.

'I have never been on stage before,' I say, weakly. 'You shouldn't trust me.'

'We should let the teacher decide that. If your aunt feels you're good enough, then you're good enough. And you should trust her, if not yourself, because she taught you well.'

I chew my lip. After five minutes of silence and realizing they aren't about to quit chasing after my choreographer, I say I'll let them know by tomorrow morning.

When they leave, I sit on a chair and squint up at Darshak. 'What do you think?'

'I think I'd love to see my girlfriend on stage.' He takes

a seat next to me and speaks after what seems like an eternity. He places his hand on my lap and draws round circles on my knee with his thumb, sending a tingling sensation through my body. 'She has always been working in the dark. Now she should walk into some light.'

I smile. He pulls me close, into his arms and kisses my temple. The touch of his soft lips calms my thoughts. 'And you'll live through the genuine fun of being up there and entertaining a screaming crowd.'

I clasp our hands together. I like the way it fits so perfectly in his. 'You are familiar with that feeling. It comes naturally to you, just like being backstage comes naturally to me.'

'Everything takes time. I was a beginner once.' He points our clasped hands at himself. 'And I think everyone will agree you have the spark. You've just never worked enough at it. Besides,' he adds, 'you never know until you try, right? And if it is Cecelia who is going to teach you, then you must try it.'

I absorb his words. It feels like a gamble. I want to please Darshak and Cecelia, but there is a huge chance I might embarrass them rather than make them, or my dance group, for that matter, proud in any way. And maybe…

Hold on. *My* dance group? The thought pops in so swiftly that I have to stop and put my mind back on track.

When I'm still thinking about ways to slither out of this situation, Darshak nudges me. 'And by the way,' he says, smiling, 'that was one heck of a kiss.'

I snort. I drop the issue for a while and decide to focus on lectures and cheering on my band late that afternoon. Anyway, Cecelia has gone to her meeting today, so she won't be home anytime soon.

...en

...at evening. I flip through
... *America's Funniest Home*
...ls or goof ups or comical
... All I can see is Shreya's
...hope and Ritesh's lack of
... a hand. The guilt creates
... visitor in this house and

...'t manage my college life alone and that I need her every now and then to help my reputation. That isn't the case. It is just that without actually being there, Cecelia has somehow created a place for herself.

I watch as a guy on TV skates down snow and plunges into a snowman. I press the mute button on the remote. When the ruckus on screen doesn't die down, I hit the remote against my palm. The power button gets stuck and the screen goes black.

Great.

What if Cecelia doesn't want people to know about her talent? Dad never mentioned she was a trained dancer and she never said anything herself. What if she intends to keep it hush-hush and I just gave her away?

What's more, I'm the one who treated her like a burden when she first turned up and now I'm the one asking her to carry mine.

But I have to. In any case, I'm not exactly the one who needs her help, so there is no harm in asking, is there?

I promise myself this is the last time I'll call for her. With that thought, I slide onto the cold floor and put my head in my arms on the seat of the sofa.

I close my eyes for ten seconds and wake up to the sound of my phone blasting. I turn, a spasm of pain shooting through the small of my back. I find Rocky curled up into a ball near my feet, his chin resting on my heel. I pat his head and strain my eyes to look at the wall clock. An hour has passed.

I wake in panic and Rocky springs up like he's sensed an earthquake.

'Rocksy,' I say when he tries to lick my face and I pull back to avoid his slobbering tongue. 'Yeah, let's get you out of this place.'

* * *

Two hours later, I walk Rocky, meet my childhood friend who lives in the building and watch as Rocky entertains a small crowd of kids. When I return home, tired and dreaming of my mattress, I find Dad's bedroom door closed. Unlatched, but closed. And there are voices coming from behind it.

'I think it's time we tell her,' a female voice floats out from his room. I let Rocky off his leash and point at a bowl of water. He strides towards it, spreads his paws on the floor with the bowl between his legs and immerses his huge mouth in it. Meanwhile, I pause at the door to listen.

'I don't think so. Is she ready yet?'

'I think she is.' The accented voice is hard to mistake.

I frown. Cecelia has never been in my bedroom or Dad's. She thinks it is intrusive and bad mannered, but I'm pretty sure it is her voice. Who else would have a Canadian accent here anyway?

'She'll accept it now,' she says.

'I know her. She likes you, but not to the point where she'd consider you her mother. She's fond of you, maybe as a friend she dearly respects not just because of the age gap but also on account of this bond you've nurtured with her. But,' he pauses, 'I still doubt it.'

Chapter Twenty-Eight

I remain numb, my legs refusing to move. I take several minutes to organize my thoughts, which are all clogged up and hear their words again, hitting me like bullets.

'She has to eventually accept it. If we want to marry, we have to tell her, now or later. And the earlier the better.'

'I suppose.' I hear Dad's small voice followed by a sharp exhale. 'But I won't have high hopes. She's young, naïve and rebellious.'

'Considering her age, she'll hesitate and have her doubts. But she's smart and sensitive enough to identify with our situation. Not right away, perhaps, but eventually.'

'I guess you know better,' Dad mumbles and I have to inch closer to the door to catch his words. 'But I must say you did a good job with her. She looks so cheerful talking to you or about you.'

Before Cecelia gets a chance to shrug her shoulders at the 'compliment', I throw the door open, glad it isn't locked. Cecelia is wrapped in Dad's arms and they are sitting on the edge of the bed leaning against each other... on the same bed that my mother shared with him and only I was allowed in there after her.

Seeing me barge in, they break off and exchange mortified looks. The first person I see is Cecelia. She jumps to her feet and takes a step forward, her hand extended towards me. Sickened, I cringe away from her.

'I don't want a stepmom,' I say, my vision blurring. I glance back from Dad to Cecelia, their faces swimming in front my eyes. Pushing himself to his feet, Father puts an arm around Cecelia which makes my heart clench. 'I don't want another mother!'

'Neha…' He advances and I slap his hand away. For the first time, I feel Mom's absence loom like a black hole, sucking me in. All the pent up grief pours out of my system all at once and I burst into tears. Dad closes the distance between us in one quick step and pulls me into a tight hug, burying his face into my hair. I wriggle and try to break free, but he stays till I calm down. When he loosens his grip, I am exhausted, calmer, but only physically.

My mind pounds with pain and I blink several times to clear my vision. That is when Cecelia speaks up, 'Nay-ha…'

Her voice exasperates me to a point that I actually feel disgusted at her for thinking of ever replacing that one sacred place in my heart. And for treating me like some sick 'project' she needed to work on. 'You're not my mother. You'll never be my mother!'

'Neha, listen to me. Will you not listen to your dad?' His tone and the obvious favouritism make me want to cry. I feel like an outsider, someone who has little say in the entire family thing and is only expected to accept whatever has been decided a long time ago.

But before he can continue, Cecelia tugs at his shoulder, keeping her gaze steady on me. 'Neha, I need to talk to you alone. I'm not asking for your compassion or empathy or even agreement. All I'm asking for is a chance for me to explain.' She purses her lips. 'Please don't judge us, because you were not supposed to find out about it this way. It isn't as bad as it looks.'

I remember the time spent with her; rubbing burn cream on the red spots on her arms and neck after we had spent a full day out in the sun, our game of Scrabble, her teaching me the dance moves she had mastered, playing English songs during the day and singing loudly along with them.

Most of all, I remember sneaking out to meet Darshak, getting into trouble and coming out alive because of her. The moment I realized I might like her after all this flashes in front me. And I feel sick to the stomach.

Hurt and resentment gnaws at my chest. 'You took me for a ride.' I meet her eyes. I had thought she was one of those friends I could share things with, never mind the fact that she is more than twice my age.

She helped me during a crisis, encouraged me without letting me believe I owed her. She never questioned me when I went out with Darshak. I've not seen any of my friends being so open to discussing their dates with grown-ups and being cheered on to devote some time to them.

But now it all seems like it was done to get into my good books. I feel tricked. 'All those pep talks and acting as if we were best friends and telling me that I could confide in you, getting me on your side. It was all an act, wasn't it?' I demand and Cecelia starts to shake her head.

'No, it wasn't,' Dad cuts in and I shoot daggers at him with my eyes. Venomous comments come to the tip of my tongue, but I hold them back. Cecelia stops Dad from adding words and I do not like the way her hand lingers on his elbow.

Cecelia is a divorcee.

'She couldn't save her own marriage, Dad.' I tear my gaze away from their interlocked hands and meet his eyes. 'How can you expect her to take care of us?'

The moment it is out, I know I have crossed the line. But not because I grasp it myself, but because a hard smack lands on my cheek. I look up and see Dad fuming for the first time. 'Watch your tongue.'

His eyes widen at what he's done and also at what I've said. He never thought his daughter was capable of being this nasty. Cecelia hugs herself and frowns at the ground.

It is humiliating. I look at Cecelia, challenging her to laugh. But she has a concerned look on her face. She seizes my dad's hand to stop him from doing more harm.

That is when Rocky rushes into the room, his tail wagging and tongue hanging out. He circles me once and stands between the three of us, looking back and forth between us and making those soft puppy noises.

We stand there staring at each other for a few seconds, when Rocky jumps on me and makes an attempt to lick my face. I break eye contact and push Rocky's muddy paws on the floor, away from me.

I run my hand over my skin where it burns. 'Dad, you're such a traitor,' I say, my voice almost breaking. I try to block his shamed face and sprint out of the room. He betrayed my mom, and I can never forgive him for that.

'Neha…' he calls after me.

I dash into my room and slam the door as hard as I can, a part of me wanting the door to come loose. Soon after, I hear Rocky's aggressive scratching on my door. I ignore the distant pleas and urgent knocks.

Chapter Twenty-Nine

I stay in my room for the next four days. I cry, sleep, wake up, hug my mom's picture, cry some more, apologize to her and sleep some more. I shut myself off from everyone, not answering calls or pleas.

Surprisingly, neither Dad nor Cecelia knocks on my bedroom door the second day. I hear a few, faint thumps twice, but realizing I have no intention of letting them in when *they* want, the knocking dies down.

I only open the door to go to the kitchen and pull out something to eat from the refrigerator. I do that when I'm sure Dad's at work and Cecelia's either sleeping or out doing whatever she does; or at night, when both of them are asleep.

I skip college, but neither of them questions it. Cecelia doesn't have the right to. And Dad must have wanted to, but I hardly give him a chance to talk. We live in one house, but face in different directions.

At least I do.

Whenever I step out of my room to fetch water or a snack, I have my earphones plugged into my ears. I make sure the volume is loud enough that no other sound can be heard. That is how I shut my father's voice out.

He has little time to reach out to me. In the morning, he

gets ready too quickly to stand and have a chat, let alone a serious conversation that needs his complete, unwavering attention. In the night, he is dog-tired.

He knocks on my door once on the first day; it is obvious from the single tentative knock that it's him. A few bangs come at night, but I don't entertain them. The next morning, nobody knocks. I wonder if Cecelia has asked him to leave me alone. If she has, then I'm grateful.

But if she presumes I need time to accept her, then she is mistaken. I want to make them understand I have absolutely no intention of accepting anyone. This is the time I'm giving *them* to decipher my silence. Cecelia needs to realize I don't like her and that she isn't needed in the house. Being the psychic that she is, she should have grasped this by now.

That morning, Rocky and I are chilling in my room. He chews his calcium bone on my bed and I sit beside him. I have been ignoring him as well and I feel terribly guilty, knowing he is the only one who isn't against me.

Rocky was overlooked the whole of yesterday and it was only this morning that I found his bowl of water empty. He lay in his kennel looking weak and hungry. I rushed to him, apologized profusely and took him to my room to feed him his lunch.

'I'm sorry, Rock,' I say now and scratch under his ear. His tail thumps once, but he is too engrossed to acknowledge me. 'I shouldn't have locked you out. All you wanted to do was comfort me.' I kiss the top of his head gently and almost tear up. We are silent for some time. I watch him chew with all his heart, focused and content.

The bone is growing smaller and his paws find it

difficult to keep it between them. I pull it out of his grip, his face turning sad when I do, and hold it for him in front of his mouth.

I know I'm probably too young to let my father act on my wishes. But frankly, it is for his own good. What if she marries him and then divorces him after a few years? I've heard too many stories about relationships in the West. How couples are into each other for a few years, but when the love withers, they fight in court to divide their wealth. And I can't let that happen with him.

'Do you think I'm a hypocrite, Rocky?' I ask, suddenly aware how backward my thoughts sound to me. When all Rocky does is be careful not to chew off my fingers along with his bone, I sigh.

Maybe I am being backward, but my dad is vulnerable. He's strong enough to raise his own daughter single-handedly after his wife's death, but he isn't strong enough to face more heartache. And I won't ever let anyone make him go through that.

Of all the people, he should have trusted me, his daughter, enough to confide in her. I'm mad because he chose Cecelia over me each time... especially when he slapped me in front of her. For her. I thought he was being utterly disloyal to Mum and that he was heartless. How can one ever get over the death of their loved ones?

But the more time I spend alone, the more I feel my anger targeted at Cecelia. Dad is only a victim. Cecelia is the player. The manipulator. She tried to win me over knowing she wouldn't get to his heart entirely until she got to mine first. And now that she has both of us, she is ready to play her trump card and hurl the news at me.

Like hell I'd surrender.

* * *

That afternoon, I hear the main door click shut. I sit in my room scrolling through Facebook. I don't pay attention to it at first, but when I walk out to fetch some snacks some time later, I find a scrawled note on the kitchen table:

Going out for a long walk. Will eat something outside and be back by three.

I check my watch and it's twelve in the afternoon, too late for a morning walk and too early for an evening one. Besides, it's odd that Cecelia would take a three-hour walk around here, but it is a welcoming freedom. I make full use of it and walk around the house without bothering about running into her. I wish whatever she's doing stretches for more than just three hours. But much to my dismay, she is back on time.

She has the house keys, so she doesn't need to press the doorbell. I'm sitting in the living room with a packet of chips on my stomach, the light from the television flickering across me. I have curtains drawn so even if it's hot and sunny outside, the room is almost in darkness.

I look at her and I'm surprised to find her clothes are all sweaty, sticking to her body. A bag hangs from her shoulder. She slips off her slippers and looks at me. Neither of us says anything. It's odd, her sudden interest in vigorous jogging or whatever she's back from doing. But obviously, I don't ask about it.

That evening she takes a rather long nap. I hear a song playing on and on and hear something vibrate three times. First, I think it's my phone. Then I remember I've switched it off for two days now. I walk into the kitchen from where the sound is coming and find Cecelia's bag on a chair.

I make sure she's asleep in her room and dig out her iPhone. An unknown number has called her thrice and as I hold the phone up, it's still ringing. It isn't Dad's number, which is a relief, but the number still looks familiar. I don't pick it up. I get the urge to access her call log and check how many times Dad and she have called each other and for how long, but I suppress it.

It's odd, though, that an Indian number other than my dad's would call her. She doesn't really know anyone in Mumbai. Or does she?

'Want something?'

I jump at the sound of her voice and drop the phone on the floor. I stare at her like a deer caught in the headlights. She narrows her eyes and picks her phone up, keeping her eyes on me.

'It has a pretty irritating ringtone,' I say in my defence, praying I sound indifferent, which is really how I feel; except, for a moment, I was distracted and became a tad bit curious about her secret social life.

Without saying anything, she checks her phone for the number and her eyes narrow. She doesn't look at me when she opens the main door and walks out of the house to attend to the call.

Out of the house.

To attend to a call.

That's very strange, but a thought I haven't had before crosses my mind. She has quite a few colleagues from the office now. It must be one of them. When she re-enters the house, I hear the last few words she utters into the phone.

'Yes I'll do it from home now, Geeta. Just add a clause at the end. That will be fine.'

Of course, Geeta Aunty. That's all I need to satisfy my curiosity.

* * *

The next morning I find another note. This time the duration of her 'walk' seems to have increased. I find the note on the kitchen table as soon as I wake up. She had left long before I woke, like Dad.

Will be going for a walk, then to office.

Will eat outside and be back by five.

I don't know why she insists on writing these useless notes. It's not like I really care what she's up to. Maybe I should write a note to her in return to tell her to do whatever she wants and that I don't need to know. But then a more vicious thought pops into my mind.

The next morning, I write a note to her in return while she takes a bath. I make sure Dad's out of the door before I do it. I scribble the note, tuck it under a glass on the kitchen table, like Cecelia does, and go back to my room to get a little more sleep. When I wake up, there is no note from her this time. Just mine—read and lying on the table, crumpled.

It reads:

You know. I don't really care if you make it home alive at the end of the day. So save yourself the trouble.

Chapter Thirty

The next morning, which is Thursday, when I don't find any sign of Cecelia in the house for about an hour after I wake up, I stand outside her closed bedroom, my ear to the door, trying to hear any sounds coming from inside. When I hear nothing, I nudge the door open, ready to defend myself if she finds me snooping. But the room is empty and so is her bathroom. The bathroom is also dry, which means she has been gone for some time now.

It's eleven in the morning, two hours since Dad left. Without dwelling too much on the thoughts creeping into my mind, I grab the house keys and run down the stairs. I go around our newly-painted building and find our watchman guiding a man to reverse his car from the parking lot. I wait for him, watching him make vigorous hand gestures and the man pokes his head out to avoid hitting other cars.

When he safely pulls out his car, he gives me a smile on his way. 'All good, Neha?'

'Yes, Uncle,' I say. 'How are you doing?'

'All good. Haven't seen you around lately.'

'Yeah. Just been busy with college.'

'Visit us some time,' he says, handing his ticket to the watchman. The ticket that marks his territory in the parking spot he just emptied. 'At least to taste your favourite *achaar*.'

I return the smile. 'Definitely.'

When his car disappears around the corner, I whirl to face the watchman. '*Bhaiyya*, did you see the foreign woman who has come to stay with us walk out from here?' I ask in Hindi and our conversation continues in that language.

He looks surprised by the sudden question. 'The white woman?'

'Yes.'

'She left a long time ago.' He squints at his watch. 'At around eight.'

At eight. That's three hours ago. 'And do you know what kind of clothes she was wearing?'

'Now, I didn't see that much.' He scratches his head. 'I guess it was something blue. Like a dress.'

'So she wore a dress? Like a flow-y, long dress?' I ask, aware of his weird looks.

'Yes,' he says. I draw in a breath, unable to wrap my mind around the idea. She wore a flowy, loose dress for her daily jogging that stretched for impossible hours. 'And was she wearing sports shoes or sandals?'

The watchman makes a face. 'I'm here to see your safety. Now who wears what, how will I know?'

I sigh. 'Okay. Never mind. And Dad left at nine, right? As usual?'

'Yes.' He points towards his right to show me our empty parking spot, which is unnecessary. 'I guided him out from there myself. But why do you ask?'

'No reason,' I say and don't wait to acknowledge his suspicious looks. I return home, pick up my phone and make a call to the office.

'Hello, is Mr Ranade there in the office? I'm Neha, his daughter,' I say, before the lady can give an elaborate, boring introduction of herself and the firm, ending with an offer to help.

'Oh.' She sounds thrown off. 'One second,' she says, replacing the phone. I wait for a few seconds before she's back on the line. 'Yes. He arrived at ten. Do you want me to put you across to him?'

'Oh, no. That's fine,' I say, heaving a sigh. 'Just don't tell him I called. I'll call him during the lunch break. Don't tell him.'

'Oh-kay,' she says tentatively. When I hang up, I throw my phone on the couch and collapse on it, pressing my thumb and forefinger to my eyes. I don't know what's wrong with me and why I'm keeping tabs and behaving like a suspicious, distrusting, freak of a daughter. I trust Dad. Of course, I do.

It's Cecelia I don't trust. If she's not with my father, then where is she? Or, what if Dad has told the receptionist to lie to people calling him, so he can hang out with her?

Hold on. That's a possibility. I pick my phone up again and dial the first number in the call log.

'Actually,' I say the second she picks up. 'I changed my mind. I want to talk to him.'

'Um,' the girl is lost again. Everything sounds very quiet on her end. 'May I please know who this is?'

'Neha, Mr Ranade's daughter,' I say, sitting straight in my seat. 'I want to speak with him. Can you put me across?'

'One second.' She is back on the line after a minute. 'Mr Ranade is in a meeting right now. He can't attend to any calls for at least an hour.'

That's all I wanted to hear. Or rather, didn't want to.

'Okay. Thanks,' I say and hang up.

About two hours later, I see my dad calling my phone. I don't pick up any of his calls. An hour later, Cecelia is back home.

Chapter Thirty-One

That evening, I find her sitting on one of the chairs in the kitchen, her legs propped up, soft sunlight pouring in through the window. The pages of *The Time Traveller's Wife* flutter in her hand under that furiously spinning fan. She smoothens out the page, pausing for a second to glance up at me. We're locked in each other's gaze for a few seconds.

Her eyes don't leave mine until I turn away first. Her lips move; she's probably saying something, but I can't hear her in my music-on, world-off mode. Not that I bother to know what she has to say. I pull a bottle of water from the refrigerator. I stride past her to my room, feeling her eyes follow me, and close the door with a thud.

* * *

It is the fifth day and I still haven't attended college. I know Darshak must be fretting. He must have tried to call a hundred times. I have to know what is going on in college in my absence, so I finally switch my phone on.

No more hiding now, I decide. I'm done with that.

I have thirty missed calls, a couple of long messages in my inbox and more than a hundred WhatsApp messages. Without tampering with the messages, I access the call notifications and find more than a dozen calls from Shreya, the girl from the underdog dance group. There are two calls from Tanna Ma'am, a few from Purti and the remaining from Darshak. I decide to call Tanna Ma'am first just to get done with what she has to say. Darshak and I would take more than an hour to catch up.

'Hello, Ma'am,' I say when she picks up my call on the third ring. 'Neha Ranade here.'

'Neha! Are you in college?'

'No Ma'am. I'm not keeping well and the doctor has advised me to take complete bed rest, so I couldn't attend college.' That lie comes out smoother than I had imagined.

'Yes. I couldn't reach you either on the phone or in person. Then somebody told me you're not holding auditions or working because you're unwell. Never mind that, though. Health's a priority.'

'Sorry Ma'am.' Who had told her I was not well? 'You had called?'

'Yes. Rachael Biswas contacted me yesterday. She said she was replacing one of her very good friends and so, she wouldn't charge us a penny.'

'That's great, Ma'am,' I say, genuinely pleased. 'Congratulations to us.'

'Yes. Thank you for that.'

'My pleasure, Ma'am.' I'm sincerely glad to hear that. At least something good materialized from Cecelia's visit.

Her name makes me ball my fist.

'So you take care. And you'll be receiving our guest. So get better by then, will you?'

'I will,' I smile.

'And don't worry if you can't work around here for a few days. Meeta will handle it.' I work under Meeta, the senior who barks orders at us and detests it when we take a breather between the unending tasks.

'Thank you, Ma'am.'

The instant I hang up, I dial Darshak's number.

Chapter Thirty-Two

The conversation kicks off before I even start to say hello.

'Neha, what the heck! Where in the world are you? And why was your freaking phone switched off?' His voice rises with every syllable, dropping a notch at the last question. 'Is everything all right?'

'Yeah.' I brush my desk with a piece of an old, torn top. Ignored for three days, it bathes in a thin layer of dust. 'I'm home. Resting.'

'Why didn't you call me?' He sounds desperate, concerned and a little angry all at the same time. I shut my eyes.

'I... I'm not well.' I hate to lie to him, but I also can't tell him the truth. I don't want him to think wrongly about my daddy. I've pledged honesty to him, but giving him a chance to judge my father is too much of a price to pay. Circumstances test your loyalty. And mine lies foremost with my only family.

'What happened?' His tone softens.

'Viral fever.' I fake a cough, which soon turns into a real fit when dust slips into my wind pipe.

'Did you see a doctor?' he asks after I calm down. I pinch the tip of my nose to hold the sneeze in. 'And why didn't you let me know? A text, a call. I could have...'

'What? Cured me?' I ask, rubbing my palm over my nose. His concern gets on my nerves a little.

'No. I'd have come to see you.'

'I'm sorry. I, ah, didn't feel like talking to anyone. Don't feel bad, but I wanted to be left alone.' I hit my elbow on a nail and wince without letting a sound out. 'You know how it is when you're bedridden with a fever. All I did all day was sleep, eat, watch TV and sleep some more.'

There is a pause. 'But a message at least,' he says. 'How hard is that? And to top it, every damn person I met who knows we have a thing going asked me about you. I hated to say I didn't know.'

'I'm sorry.' I know I sound low, I *feel* low. But fever is the best reason for getting away with the sadness and gloom that absorbs me.

I hear him exhale sharply. 'Don't be.'

Silence. 'I called Tanna Ma'am,' I say after a while, ducking out from under the table and inhaling the fresh air. 'How come she already knew I was unwell, since you're the first person I told right now?'

'Because I spread the rumour,' he mumbles. 'I didn't know where you were, so I said you were down with fever.' I smile, arranging the books so they're upright in one corner of my table. 'Now I know it's the truth though,' he says. 'Should I come to your house?'

'No!' I say a bit too quickly, toppling the stack of books I had neatly arranged. 'I mean I'm fine. I'll meet you tomorrow anyway,' I say and let the books stay in a heap. I collapse on the bed and hug my pillow.

I don't want to prolong this conversation about my

health. If he delves into any more details, I know I won't come up with stories fast enough. 'Chuck that. Any updates?'

'Yeah. Our practice is going well and that's that,' he says, trying but failing to sound cheerful. 'Are you really all right, Neha? I mean not keeping well is the only reason you bunked college?'

Why is he being so pushy? I want to curtail this conversation before I say something I shouldn't.

'Yeah, obvio. Do you doubt me?' I don't wait for a reply. 'Can I call you back later, baby? My head feels like it'll crack open any minute,' I say and make a sick rumble deep in my throat. 'I need a nap.'

'Sure. Take care, bud.'

'Love you,' I mutter and hear him say, 'You too,' before hanging up.

I sigh and without warning, a fresh set of tears pour out of me. I stare at the photo album lying open at the foot of my bed. In the picture on top, I'm sitting in my mom's arms like that is where I belong, while she claps along to Ganpati *aarti*.

An odd feeling of emptiness swirls in my heart. This sadness was buried deep within me for all these years. It was only so well shielded behind luxury and pampering that I never really realized just how deep the grief was; the grief of losing a mother, an indispensable and irreplaceable part of your life.

I hug my mom's picture and decide to take a nap before calling anyone else who had left missed calls.

Chapter Thirty-Three

When I wake up after about an hour to a scraping sound, which is only Rocky trying to dig a hole in the marble tiles of my room, I swipe my phone open. Another three missed calls from Purti and I spring up in my bed. I swipe on her name and hold the phone to my ear.

'Hey Purti,' I say when she picks my call up on the first ring. I rest my head on the wall and let my feet dangle from the edge of the bed. I shush Rocky to stop him from scuffing the wall paint. 'I'm sorry for not calling. I was not…'

Sniffle.

'Purti?'

Another sniffle. I hear a rustle on the other end and then, sniffling. I frown.

'Pop. Are you fine?' I shoot up in my bed. I rub my eyes and my hands reach for the nearest top I can throw on. 'Are you crying?'

'Hey bud.' Her voice shakes. I know her too well not to make out that something is wrong.

'Purti what happened?'

'Nothing.' She giggles. 'Listen I was thinking of buying new track pants for this coming trek.'

I balance my phone between my shoulder and ear while

I try to squeeze into my pants. I pause to reply. 'Ah. For… for the trek?'

'Yeah!' She giggles again. 'I don't fit into the old ones anymore. Have I gained weight?'

'Are you drunk?' My jaw drops open.

'Am I too fat?'

'Shut up and answer me.'

'Maybe a bit.'

'Where are you?'

'Nowhere.'

'There's no place called nowhere.'

'That's the point. I don't know where I am. If I ever was.'

'What are you saying, Pop? Tell me where you are.'

'I seriously don't know. Wait I'll ask someone… 'Cuse me? Excuse me, sir. Hello sir. What? I'm too ugly for you to wait and have a chat? To hell with you! I can sing the shit out of you!'

'Purti!'

She starts to sing *Awari* and for a second I pause, holding my breath at the notes that she hits. This girl is crazy—crazily talented.

I want to yell at her over the phone. Ask her for directions to wherever she is sprawled in her misery and yank her out of there. But I can't help but stand in silence, mesmerized by her voice. The chattering on her end quietens, as if everyone has stopped talking to listen to her sing.

'Purti, hold on for a tick till I talk to Darshak, okay?' I

say into the phone when she pauses to take a breath, but to no avail. She starts to sing the next stanza, forgetting I'm on the other end. I put her on hold and make a second call.

'Darshak!' I say as soon as the ringing stops and he has picked up. 'Purti has lost it. I need you to find out where she is. Ask her dumb boyfriend. Navigate or send cops to her. But FIND HER!'

There is silence.

'Darshak, you better speak up.'

'Neha, I thought you knew.'

My heart beats so fast it seems to be break dancing in my ribcage. 'What?'

'Purti and her boyfriend broke up three days ago.'

Silence. Now on my end.

'Neha. I know you—' I cut his call before I can hear him finish his sentence. I put Purti back on the line. I close my eyes and listen to her, the back of my eyes starting to sting.

'Purti,' I whisper, but I'm sure she doesn't hear me. She is busy saying, 'Thank you,' over and over again. It seems people are congratulating her. When the voices die down, I hear her sigh.

'Purti...'

'Don't,' she says, her voice hoarse. 'Don't you dare say you told me so.'

'I won't. Will you tell me where you are?' I ask softly. I want to go and comfort her wherever she is, but I won't press her this time. If she wants me there with her, she'll tell me.

'No,' is all she says and we're silent for a long time.

'Are you drunk?'

'Maybe a little.'

'Why didn't you...' I start to say, but stop myself. I can't ask her why she didn't tell me. My phone had been off for the past four days. 'I'm sorry.'

She laughs. 'Why are you saying sorry?'

'I wasn't there when you needed me the most.'

She doesn't say anything. Then I hear her sniffle. 'The more I think about it now, the more obvious it seems. He was hardly there when I had a real problem, but magically appeared when everything was going well. Always asked me to sing for his friends. Actually…' she scoffs, 'that is the only time I saw him look at me like I was magic. When I sang.'

'That's 'cause you *are* magic when you sing. You just need to find someone who will think you're magic when you wake up in the morning with messy hair or cry or eat or burp. You need to find someone who will celebrate you the way you are and not just occasionally.'

She is quiet. After about a minute, she speaks, 'Do you think he dumped me because I'm ugly?'

'No. He dumped you because he was a jerk. And I bet he'll come crawling back to you once he realizes he's lost the real deal, chasing plastic dolls.'

She absorbs my words, or so I suppose, and sighs. 'I don't think I can perform at our annual.'

'Pop, no. You need to snap out of it. I told you he wasn't the right person for you. Nobody liked him. And I feel it isn't him, it's you who needs to raise her dating standards.

Don't let people like him stop you from singing,' I tell her, suddenly terrified she will drown her misery in drinks and never sing again. I tell her she can't sit there all day and night crying about moving on. She can mourn all she wants after the show. Now isn't the time.

There is a long silence.

'Snap out of it. Raise my standards. Mourn all I want after the show.' She repeats my words in a monotone. I'm heartless enough to voice them aloud. But it is a fact, isn't it?

'Wow. That was,' she pauses. Her voice is almost a whisper, 'brutal.'

'Purti...'

'You know? You're just an insensitive, self-centred girl. As long as people behave the way you want, you're okay. I don't know why I even thought you'd understand me,' she snorts. 'And raise my standards? Do you even know what I shared with him? Even if it was nothing, you have no right to judge!'

'I didn't—'

'Why did you call anyway? After all the storms calmed down. I just said I can't sing *once* and you're all panicky. As if that is all there is to me. Can't you say I need not worry just for the sake of it?' Her voice rises and she almost shouts the last sentence to everyone around her, 'Is there anyone who truly cares about me and not just my freaking talent?'

I try to look past her words. She is upset. She doesn't mean them.

'Pop, you *are* your…,' I start but hear a click on the other end. 'Talent,' I close my eyes and finish to a dead line.

Chapter Thirty-Four

The next day in college, I sit next to Darshak in our lecture. Purti has exited our chat group. After sending off a dozen messages and calls, I find out I've been blocked and my calls have been added to the reject list on her phone. I think back to last night's conversation and realize what I had said was true, only she was too vulnerable to listen to it.

I run my hand across my face, exhausted and not registering a single word the teacher speaks. Last night, I saw Dad sitting in the kitchen scrolling through the pages of the British Airways website on his laptop. I tried to peep in, but didn't want to risk coming face to face with him. So I hid in my room and waited till he stretched his arms over his head, turned off the laptop and walked into his room before I went out and fetched water.

He looked tired and his steps were dragging, like he was forcing himself to work or walk. Seeing him like that kept me up half the night, tossing and turning in my bed.

I squeeze my intertwined fingers between my knees. I wish I could just stop that dull ache in my heart. I can't even tell what is causing it anymore.

'So what have you decided?' Darshak asks and I almost jump, startled. He creeps closer to me, so that the big, fat guy sitting on the front bench blocks him from sir's view.

I remind myself I'm in a classroom and collect my

thoughts which are swirling around Dad and Purti. 'About what?' I ask.

'About the dance.' He looks at me sideways. 'I just told you I got calls from Shreya last night asking for your decision.'

I furrow my brows while I stare at the numbers on the blackboard. That girl was still around? 'How did she get your number?'

'That's not the point. The point is...'

Sir whirls around to look at the class and narrows his eyes. He probably can't figure out the source of the sound, but suspects someone is talking. We straighten in our seats. When he faces the blackboard again, Darshak resumes talking. 'She couldn't reach you and so she called me. Are you going to help her or not?'

I doodle something in the top right corner, which is meant to look like a flower. 'I haven't decided.'

'Then please decide.' He places his hand on mine, stopping me from shading the petals. 'There're hardly any days left for them to practice.'

'Why are you advocating for her so much?'

Darshak glances down at me from the corner of his eye. I flick his hand away and tint the leaves with black ink. He shakes his head, the corner of his mouth turning up. 'I'm just saying. I don't want her to disturb me again tonight. And come to think of it, they've only got about a week to get their shit together.'

'She's going to call you again?' I ignore the point of the argument and let my possessiveness take over.

I should probably tell Shreya he's already taken.

'She might. Seeing how desperate she is to get selected, she might as well call Cecelia directly.'

'What is going on there?' Sir booms. We swiftly part and stare into our books hard, pretending to understand a rather difficult concept. 'I can hear constant murmuring from that corner.' He narrows his eyes in our general direction. 'If you want to chit chat, then please leave the class.' A few kids around us snigger, knowing it's us. 'And if I hear a single word now, I'll start asking questions.'

That sentence washes any signs of a smile from our faces. It is one thing when he warns us, but an altogether different one when he threatens us. Pissing him off at the very moment he threatens to ask questions is a bit more life-threatening than throwing yourself into water swarming with hungry sharks. He never simply asks questions and insults the students who are unable to answer. He makes sure he asks precisely those questions we'd be unable to answer. So to save everyone from losing face we silently decide to postpone our conversation.

'If Shreya calls you again tell her you don't know anything. Don't entertain her, okay?' I tell Darshak when we head to the bus stop that evening after college.

'Are you worried she might steal me from you?' He wriggles his brows.

'What? Not at all.'

'Then worried about the fact that she will call me again?'

'No. Why would that worry me? I'm just trying to help you get her off your back.'

'But I never said she was on my back.' He kicks a pebble

on the street. It hits the heel of someone walking ahead of us. I know Darshak is merely messing around, but I'm not in a mood to laugh it off. I look anywhere but at him.

'Listen.' He turns to face me. 'The point is not how she got her hands on my number or if she will call again. The point is whether you want to help them or not. You shouldn't leave them hanging like that.'

'She came to me. I didn't go to her. So why is there this pressure on me?' I ask, irritated.

'It's not about pressure, Neha. It's about being reliable and mature.'

'You mean I'm not?'

'Did I say that?'

'Why are you bending over backwards for her? If you're so into her, then *you* choreograph their dance. Or better, go sleep with her!'

'Watch your tongue, Neha.' Suddenly serious, his voice drops low. Dad's face flashes in front of me. 'Watch your tongue,' he'd said when he sided with Cecelia. Apparently, everybody is teamed up with the people I'm against. I feel a lump rising in my throat. 'I'm not asking you to help them. I'm just saying answer them. Yes or no, it doesn't matter. They are counting on you.'

'I'll talk to her,' I murmur.

'Don't talk. Be direct and get this over with.'

'I said I'll talk to her! Give me a damn break and just get the hell out of my system, you people!' I turn on my heel. 'And if you want to help the damsel in distress then really, you're free to break the hell up with me.'

Our mates walking in front of us pause to look back. Darshak raises his hand, gesturing for them to keep walking.

'You don't have to tell me what to do and what not to. Let me figure it out myself, will you?' I say and hail a cab without glancing back to see if he is following. I want to be left alone and I can't bear the thought of spending the next hour with him, or anyone else.

Frankly, I don't care. I don't care if he follows me or not. I don't care if Shreya and her dance group get selected or not. I don't care if that star comes to our function or not. I don't care if the annual function is a hit or not. And I seriously don't care if my dad remarries or not.

I wipe my eyes before I reach my lane.

Chapter Thirty-Five

On Saturday night, I pull down my rucksack from the cupboard and dust it off. It hasn't been used for four months, since the time I last went for a trek. I load it with water bottles, a long-sleeved top, an extra pair of trousers, socks, newspaper, polythene bags and packets of dry food items. I get the itch to peep into Cecelia's room to check on her, to see if she has packed the essentials. But my pride holds me back.

For the first time, I am in no mood to go on a trek. I was excited only a few days ago, but with the recent turn of events the last thing I want to do now is spend an entire day with Cecelia and Darshak. More so, when they both are on the same team and I'll be the one side-lined.

But the fees are all paid and I haven't been to this place before. As a hiker, I don't want to miss an opportunity to explore places, especially when all's paid for and planned.

Besides, Purti is going to be there. I'm positive she'll be in a better mood, since trekking is something she enjoys a lot. And I'm hoping to mend fences with her.

But most of all, I wouldn't cancel one of my favourite activities for someone who holds very little significance in my life. Not in a million years will I let Cecelia go and hang out with my friends, while I sit at home, all sad and miserable.

So at around six o'clock on Sunday morning, I pull my bag onto my back and drag my feet out. I see Cecelia and Dad waiting in the living room. Cecelia wears a faded pink running tee with an orange scarf around her neck and grey track pants. A black windcheater is tossed on her bag on the floor. The bag belongs to my dad.

'I need to have a word with you,' Dad says when he sees me enter the hallway. He gets to his feet and waves at me to follow him into his study. I drop my bag on the floor and go after him, aware of Cecelia's gaze following us.

'I don't want to lecture you, but make sure you take care of her.' He nods in the direction of the living room. 'No matter how mad you are at us, it's your responsibility—'

'When was it not?' I meet his eyes. I can see the moisture in the corners of his reddened eyes. He looks sleep deprived, like he's been disturbed in the middle of a peaceful sleep… which perhaps he has been.

Before today, he has never had to worry whether I'd wake up for one-day treks or reach safely or not. I inform him a day before leaving, write down the place and my time of return and that is that. I only had to pick my bag up and leave in the morning with one sticky note posted on the fridge that'd read something like, 'Leaving. Will be back by evening. Take care. Love you.' No more questions asked, none answered.

He knows I'm a pro. As long as I am back on time, he doesn't even bother to call. This is only because of the years of trust I have built regarding my trek schedules. And I admit this is one area where I would never break it. So far, I've maintained complete transparency and never used trekking as an excuse to sneak out. He knows I need to go on these kinds of regular excursions to rejuvenate my mind.

Maybe that is why he does not stop me from going this time around, even after having such a serious fight with me. Maybe he supposes after I'm back from paradise, I'll calm down and be rational.

I suspect Cecelia would have tried to cancel this plan as well, but going by how Dad's mind works, he'd have asked her to tag along. It might give us some time together.

Not that it matters. I have learnt how to dodge a trap. This time I wasn't going to slip.

Dad decides to ignore my snide remark. 'And I know you'll be fine. You've gone on enough treks to lead one on your own, but Cecelia hasn't.'

'Don't worry, Papa. Trekkers stick together through thick and thin. We don't abandon our mates midway or lead them on.'

I see my dad's nostrils flare before a surprise yawn suppresses his anger. He sighs, letting my statement pass. 'Just make sure you both come home in one piece.'

Not that I care, but just so Dad can sleep better, I nod. In about another half an hour, one of my friends picks us up in her car and in another half an hour, we board the bus and begin our journey.

* * *

On the three-hour drive, Cecelia sits with Darshak in one of the front seats. I see the sides of her pants and one hand resting on the armrest of her seat. She leans over occasionally to say something to Darshak. I only see the top of his head peeking out over his seat.

Purti and Shirish, another member of our band, huddle together in the back seats and whenever I turn around to check on my best friend, I find her staring at one point or the other, sometimes out the window, at the ground or at the top of the bus with her head resting back. She doesn't even blink most of the time. I fight an urge to run and comfort her. Only once during the long silent ride do I see Purti's head drop on Shirish's shoulder. He adjusts his position to make her comfortable. I'm glad she has someone, if not me.

Chapter Thirty-Six

Our journey is quiet and dull. Every time we're in the bus we're either laughing or cracking jokes, pulling each other's legs or singing at the tops of our voices. If someone is too quiet and shy, we push him to the centre and make him dance in the aisle of the moving bus. It's always been a tradition to make loners loosen up and liven up the environment.

This time though it feels like a funeral. Nobody's talking to anybody; everyone is either sleeping or staring out the window. My two best friends don't look back once to check on me. And the only extra member today is Cecelia who, like always, is the reason everything is off.

We hop off the bus when we reach our destination in three hours, gobble down our *poha* breakfast and our tour leader calls for attention. We huddle around him in a circle and I stifle a yawn as the regular round of introductions begins.

'Let's start with Neha before she dozes off,' he says and I snap to attention. I flush when faces turn to stare at me.

'I'm Neha. Been trekking for almost all my life. I study at Westwood College, first year BCom. If there's anything I love apart from trekking, it's staying busy. Doing anything but nothing.'

When a few intros are done, I hear Purti's voice. She's

wearing a cherry red t-shirt that belongs to her ex-boyfriend and khaki coloured cargo pants. I notice her hollow eyes and the unmistakable dark circles under them. She hasn't slept properly. 'I'm Purti, studying in First Year BCom at Westwood. I love singing. And trekking is therapeutic. Nothing heals you better than nature.'

Darshak nods. 'I'm Darshak studying in her class.' He points at Purti whose mouth curves slightly. 'Love singing, playing keyboard and music in general.'

I purse my lips. I'm obviously in the same class, but the two most important people in my life seem to have forgotten that. My mammoth ego is bruised. I decide to give them the cold shoulder right back.

'I'm Cecelia. I'm Neha's aunt.' Cecelia's gaze meets mine and I suddenly become more interested in a fallen branch behind her. 'I had come for some work to India, but that's done. Since I had another week or so to spare and nothing better to do, she asked me to tag along. So here I am.'

'So this is your first time?' our leader asks. When she nods, he says, 'Okay. So stick close to our leaders and inform us immediately if you feel off or anything. Okay?'

'Oh. Don't worry about me.' She smiles.

'We'll take care of her,' Darshak pipes up and Cecelia half hugs him. I'm glad they aren't looking at me or they would see smoke coming out of my ears. I don't want her associated with any of my people.

'Good.' At the end of all the introductions the leader says, 'Stick together and look out for one another. There'll be one leader in the front, one at the back and one in the middle of the group. You're not supposed to overtake the one in the front or lag too far behind the one at the end.'

We nod and with a shout, head up.

I spend the climb up getting to know the other people and keep ignoring Darshak and Cecelia. I ignore Purti by default, since all she does is hover around those two. Occasionally, I see her talk to Cecelia and if I'm not mistaken, shed a tear. Her hand reaches up to scratch the corner of her eye.

In a way I'm glad. If she finds comfort in Cecelia's words more than mine I'm all up for not interrupting their conversations.

* * *

On our way down, there is one time I accidently face Cecelia.

'Your dad.' Cecelia stretches her arm out to me and I see 'Rajeev R' flashing on her iPhone screen. We are on our way down the hill. I blink at the name once and brush past her to join the others. If I had eyes in the back of my head, I'd have seen the horrid look on her face.

'She is not around.' I hear Cecelia's voice close behind. Quite a liar. Not surprising. 'Yeah. When I spot her I'll ask her to call you. No, she's fine. We're together. It's just that I'm a slow walker and she's ahead. She's quite a hiker...'

I heard that, but I wasn't going to show that I did. Flattery isn't going to work this time. I rush ahead and wind my arm around my friend, taking steps in time with hers.

'You take the instruction 'stick together' quite literally.' She casts a look at me and I laugh a little too loudly as we pass, so Darshak (who's peering into his camera to take the perfect picture of a bored insect) can hear it.

Chapter Thirty-Seven

The next day isn't an eventful one at college. Mostly, I run errands for the function. I skip the music rehearsals. I don't want to face either of my friends and I know I won't be welcome there anyway. So I decide to leave college in the afternoon and go home and take a nap instead. That is when Shreya, the Racketeers dance member, stops me on the staircase. I knew I had to face her someday.

'Neha!'

I take a deep breath and check my temper. I wouldn't lose it at her. She was only asking for help from Darshak, because she couldn't reach me. I order my mind to stay calm. 'Yeah.'

'Um, I tried to call you so many times, but your cell was switched off. I just wanted to tell you,' she says, 'that we've started practising and we don't need a tutor any longer.'

'What?'

'We didn't hear from you for so many days and we were already running out of time. So, ah, we decided to do it ourselves.'

I blink a few times. 'So... you're saying you're choreographing the dance yourself?' I confirm. If it is true then I thank my stars for taking this one weight off my shoulders.

She looks frightened of speaking as if I'd slap her if she says something I don't want to hear. I wince at the thought. I really don't want her to be scared of me.

Sure, I'm upset and rumours spread fast. Someone must have stated I had a fight with Darshak about her, but that doesn't mean I'd go about losing it at every other person. I have a right over Darshak, so I'm allowed to behave any way I want with him. But only with him.

'Yeah. We are,' she says. 'We all decided to come up with ten unique steps each,' she explains, nervously playing with her hair. 'Like, um, we referred to YouTube videos, asked dancers we knew to show us a couple of steps and basically, stole from any available source. Then we decided to connect all those steps, or at least the best ones, and choreographed a complete dance. I mean it's still underway though, but, yeah.'

I beam. 'That's great,' I say, genuinely pleased to hear that. It is a relief to know that they finally decided to move on, because I was seriously starting to doubt if I could ever get around to helping her. She was just another problem at the very bottom of my list.

I have wanted to help her, really, from the bottom of my heart, but it wasn't just restricted to me. It required Cecelia's involvement. And I didn't want to do anything with that woman.

'I'd have loved to help you but you know, I... I mean,' I give up on explaining myself, 'Listen, I'm sorry, okay.'

'No that's fine! Totally!' She shakes her head, fidgeting with her phone now. 'If you really want to help us then there's still something you can do.'

I narrow my eyes. 'Does that involve me negotiating or charming some of the teachers so they select you? Sorry, then I can't.'

'No! It's not that. It's… well.' I have never seen her this nervous before. I put my hand on her shoulder and give it a gentle squeeze, conveying she needn't be so afraid.

'Well, I just, I mean we are… you know the girl who left us?'

I nod.

'She was Ritesh's partner. And a stupid girl. She shouldn't have ditched us last minute. But that place is still vacant and no good dancer wants to blow up their chances performing with us...' She looks at the ground, I guess fighting back tears. My heart goes out to her. Her group is the most underestimated, defeated group out there. And probably the weakest.

'So you haven't found anyone yet and as a last resort, you want me to perform in her place?' I provide softly.

She looks up, a little horrified. 'No! Not as a last resort.'

She isn't a good liar. I smile. 'I'll do it.'

She stares at me for a long time, her face unreadable, before her mouth quivers. 'You will?' She mutters something about the conversation being easier than she expected. I can't help but laugh. Seeing me so relaxed, she breaks into a grin.

'Thank you.' She suddenly launches herself at me for a hug. Her uneven breathing is filled with sniffs and her bushy hair pricks my face. I pat her.

'You're welcome.'

Now that I've made a person happy for the first time and not teary eyed or angry, I'm terrified more than ever. It's so much easier to live in my selfish world and let people deal with my shit than go out and actually help them.

I promised her, but how do I keep the promise? Will I be able to catch up as fast as they can? Dancers pick up steps faster than the rest of us and they do it gracefully.

What if I freeze on stage? What if I go blank? What if I can't learn a single thing they try to teach me?

After about half an hour, I push past a fat man blocking my way into the bus. His weight squashes me to a side when the bus jerks to a start. He apologizes and I stagger to my feet. As the thoughts swirl in my mind, I feel stuck between a rock and a hard place.

Chapter Thirty-Eight

The next morning Cecelia is gone before Dad is out of the house. God knows what she is up to. But that gives me a moment with him to talk. Even though I'm mad at him, it's very rare that I get to spend alone time with him without that woman hovering around us these days. So I decide to take advantage of this opportunity.

'Hey,' I say when I see Dad tugging on his shoes to leave for office. I'm still in my pyjamas and I haven't brushed yet.

He looks up and is surprised to find me awake this early. Or maybe he's surprised I'm talking to him.

'Hey.' He smiles. And then he says too much too fast, probably scared I might run away any second. 'I have your pocket money tucked into my coat pocket if you need. And I didn't have much time to prepare your favourite breakfast today, so I made *sheera*. Cecelia liked it when we had it in the office the other day, so I thought maybe...' he trails off, perhaps realizing he's talking about the person who's caused all the problems.

I try to smile. 'It is fine, Papa.' I don't point out that I'm not a huge fan of *sheera*. 'How are your days going?'

His voice drops. 'Without my only daughter talking to me? Fine, I guess.'

'Good.' I don't know what else to say. There is so much

to be said, so much to be resolved that neither of us knows where to start. So we stick to small talk.

'You...' he starts and then clears his throat. 'Did you sleep well?' I have a feeling this is not what he set out to ask.

'With my real mother haunting my dreams and crying because she feels we don't need her anymore? Fine, I guess.'

He is visibly uncomfortable. Then he says, 'Cecelia will be back for lunch today. She's taken to jogging lately.'

'I gathered that.'

'Why don't you go with her?'

I stare at him for a very long time. I really can't believe he just said that to me when he knows exactly how I feel about her. The fact that I just talked about my mother and he's still directing every conversation back towards Cecelia is just too much for me to handle. I guess it was a mistake to try and talk with him after all.

'I mean only if you want to. It' not like she'll be—'

'I have to go to the bathroom. I'll see you, Dad,' I say and rush into my room. I lock the bathroom door. He calls once and I can hear him waiting outside my bathroom for some time, probably waiting for me to come out.

'I didn't mean it that way,' he says through the closed door. I'm standing right by the door on the inside, so close I can hear his breathing along with his words. 'What I mean is you shouldn't part ways with people on a bitter note. It's...'

'I know you both have been meeting secretly,' I interrupt him and say, although not in a mean way. But I need him to know that I'm aware. 'So please go to her. She must be waiting.'

'What? Why would I meet her outside when I see her at home every day?' he asks.

'Isn't that obvious, Papa?' I smile, the smile not reaching my eyes. 'So that I'm not around.'

'Neha, that's rubbish. From where does your mind come up with...' he starts, launching into an explanation. I suddenly remember I have my phone in my pyjama pocket. I pull it out and play the first song on my list on loud. I run the tap water just to add to the noise and drown his words.

'Neha?' he calls out much louder this time, but his voice is too soft to be heard over the rap song. I guess he gets the message. After about ten minutes, I hear his feet shuffle outside and the main door click shut.

I press my head to the bathroom door and close my eyes. This is getting harder by the day.

* * *

That afternoon I don't wait for Cecelia to get home. Apart from the obvious reason that I can't stand her even more after my failed encounter with Dad, I have something more productive to do in college than to wait around for orders from seniors or ignore my best friends.

I have my own dance practice to look forward to. And somehow the thought of having people around who I've never been acquainted with and letting out pent up energy to create art sounds liberating.

I tentatively enter the classroom at around two in the afternoon as Shreya had told me. Benches are pushed to the wall and a Bluetooth speaker is placed on a chair in front of the room. The speaker plays an English song I don't recognize.

I look at the dancers in the room: five boys and four girls. Surprisingly they're dancing without uttering a single word against one another. Ritesh is the only one dancing without a partner and he looks funny doing all those couples' steps alone. I observe them for some time.

The girls jog two steps forward and leap onto their partners. They hold their heads up for a second and land on their feet in a swift motion. I catch my breath as if I've swallowed a peach seed.

Am I expected to do that?

'Neha!' someone says. It's Shreya. She notices me standing by the door and stops the music. When she has everyone's attention, she does a round of introductions. I only bother to remember Ritesh's name, since he's going to be my partner for the next few days.

One of the guys crumples to the floor like a dried leaf and leans his back against the legs of a bench. 'I'm taking a damn break.'

'So am I,' a girl says and collapses on a bench.

'Sorry.' Shreya shrugs at me. 'Both dance studios are engaged. They're only free for two hours in the morning and two in the evening. We'll shift our dance there in about…' she squints at her watch, 'two hours. Adjust here, till then.'

I nod mechanically, the lifts and their grace haunting my mind. I can never match up to that awesomeness.

'Let's start with some stretching,' Ritesh tells me. I see the other couples lean against the nearest wall. I lift a brow, unsure what is happening.

'It'll make your muscles a little flexible before we shock them with the dance steps,' he says. I see a girl raise her leg high and plop it effortlessly on her partner's shoulder. He clutches her elbows and rises slowly to maintain her balance. Her leg is now in a perfect vertical split.

'Your turn.' I don't realize my mouth is open. When Ritesh asks me to copy them, I gulp.

And they say they are the least talented of all.

* * *

At the end of that day, my muscles ache and that is when Ritesh decides to blast me with the information. 'Bring heels from tomorrow.'

'Heels?' I ask in a daze.

'You'll dance in heels,' he says, pulling his socks up.

'But... but I don't have heels.' My voice is small, barely audible.

'Buy, steal, beg, borrow. No heels, no practice.' He hops and waves at everyone in the room. 'Catch you guys tomorrow.'

I have seen two-inch red pencil heels on our shoe rack at home, obviously belonging to Cecelia. But the last thing I'd do is ask her for help.

'Don't worry. I'll get you one,' Shreya says. 'Temporarily. Buy a pair as soon as you can.'

I sigh in relief. 'Thank you.'

* * *

The next seven days, I work on auto pilot mode. I do not worry about remembering all the steps, because it only makes me want to run in the opposite direction. I focus on just one chunk of it at a time.

I almost die every afternoon stretching and exercising in the first hour of our practice, but somehow doing that makes the dance seem easier.

The days demand all my energy and mental strength. I grab sandwiches, puffs, frankies or whatever I can find on my way home and eat them in the bus. By the time I crawl home and into my bed at night, I have no energy to think about anything else but my sleep. These days even Mum has stopped visiting my dreams. Maybe she realizes I need all the peace and rest I can get.

On weekends, we assemble at Ritesh's place, which is less of an apartment and more of a mansion, and practise for thirteen hours. Yes, thirteen. No kidding. At the end of the rehearsal day, when everybody is working on the steps they are not good at and Ritesh and I are practising our air-catch, I tell him, 'I don't know much about the technicality of dance, but I really love this.'

A small, rare smile touches his lips.

'No really. You guys underestimated your own creativity.' I feel the need to say this, because I'm truly proud of my group. And especially say this to Ritesh, because he seems pouty and angry most of the time. 'You shouldn't have waited till every person on this planet refused to teach you to take matters in your hands and teach yourself. It doesn't matter if it was only through YouTube videos and a bit of outside help.'

Ritesh and two more dancers who're practising near us stop and stare at me. For a second, I fear I've hurt them by reminding them that nobody wanted to teach us.

'I'm sorry,' I say. 'I didn't mean to bring the past up.'

Ritesh clears his throat. 'It's okay. And yeah, ah, we did teach ourselves pretty well.' He looks over at the two dancers who smile and go back to their dance routine. Before starting to practise, I put a hand on Ritesh's shoulder, assuring him everything will be fine. And that we deserve this more than anyone else.

* * *

Surprisingly, Darshak doesn't bug me throughout. I regret not telling him what's going on in my life. He really has no clue, but the sessions wear me down. Somehow, I have a feeling he's aware of my involvement with the dance team, what with Shreya being a part of it. And he still hasn't bothered me, which is a welcome relief. His calls would only mess with my focus.

Cecelia still jogs and goes to office. I guess she's too bored of staying home and doing nothing; the after effect of a successful meeting means less work for her. Or maybe she just can't stand me the same way I can't stand her, so she's away the whole morning and I stay in bed long enough that I don't see Dad leave home.

Purti seems to have disappeared from this planet. I haven't seen her anywhere. But if Darshak knows about me, I know she does too. And I mentally thank them both for not bothering me.

* * *

I practise every waking second of next week. When I'm eating or answering nature's call, I retrace all the steps in my mind. During lectures, I envision myself as well as my team members pirouetting. In the shower, I twirl. While peeing, I practise the expressions best suited to the dance. Not a minute passes when I'm not thinking about it.

There are a couple of reasons I'm so obsessed with getting everything right. The steps are demanding and at times daunting, but worth making the effort for, all the same. And second, I'm the weakest member on the team.

Despite this fact, my team encourages and motivates me without fussing about me being a slow learner or an average dancer. They appreciate my efforts and let me know I'm improving. Sometimes I feel like we're one huge snowball with some crazy motivational force rolling us down the hill.

Ritesh is a pretty good partner, easy to follow and trust. My first impression of him was that he was always mean to people, that he never smiled, was perpetually angry at the world and stuck to himself most of the time. The image isn't wrong at all. He hardly speaks with me and his curt tone makes us feel he'll lose it any time, but he's a good guide.

I'm not much into the choreography thing, since I hardly give any input. So they have come up with an interesting plan. Since I have the other department work I can't ditch, I attend to that in the late morning and join the Racketeers in the mid-afternoon. When I'm not around they come up with steps, teach me and we practise as soon as I join them.

Everything feels so perfect, I fear this might be taken away from me any minute. So I slog to keep my teammates' belief in me alive by being sincere. I've also stopped fuelling gossip about how weak the Racketeers are. Not because I'm a part of it now, but because those rumours are just that. Rumours.

Chapter Thirty-Nine

Thursday is the selection day. The dance we perform that day, if selected, will be finalized for the function on Saturday. There is no time to perfect our moves after the selection. If we fail to impress the judges now, we're out. But a fact that lessens my dread is that the teachers on the judging panel are all familiar with me. I've helped them audition other students and in a way, that is a confidence booster.

When we enter the auditorium I look at Tanna Ma'am and she nods at me.

Ritesh and I position ourselves in the second row at the back. Ritesh is one of the dancers with a sharp memory and is usually placed in front. But I wanted to avoid being in the direct spotlight, so on my request, we are at the back.

When we face the nearly empty auditorium, I spot Darshak and the others, except Purti, sitting in the back seats. Darshak gives me an inconspicuous thumbs-up. I smile.

Ritesh squeezes my hand and glances at me sideways. 'We'll do it.'

The music begins and he whispers, 'One, two three, four,' for us to hear. I hear a few claps in the audience. Tanna Ma'am clicks her tongue and waves from the front desk to silence them.

I fill my lungs with a deep breath till my mind clears of the dizziness. Once the music begins I grasp the rhythm. I move in time with the others and I manage to do it without being rooted to the ground. We nail the catch and I can't help but smile at Ritesh in the middle of our dance. I hear a few claps reverberate in the auditorium.

I get two steps terribly wrong, making Ritesh lose his balance as well, but nobody seems to notice it. When our dance ends we bow and Darshak stands up first to cheer.

The judges barely smile. I doubt they even liked us.

But before they call the next group, Tanna Ma'am smiles at me. It is almost an invisible smile, but that is enough for me to know that we have made it.

When they summon us to break the news that we are in, we walk out of the cabin jumping and punching the air and high-fiving one another.

I see Darshak waiting for me by the elevator. The moment my gaze falls on him I run and leap up onto him. It is a long, bear hug with my feet off the ground. I can feel his breath in my hair.

I haven't disappointed the people who counted on me and I haven't disappointed myself. I shed a tear or two for our selection and some for going berserk on him, burying my face in his shoulder. I try to somehow convey my guilt and an unspoken apology through that embrace.

Not that he needs it.

'Congrats,' he says when we pull away, and smiles. I stand close enough to smell his minty breath. 'You made it.'

I gaze at his lips and then into his eyes. 'Kiss me.'

He raises his brows and flicks a glance behind me. 'Here?'

I shrug, staring at him. He seizes my arm so hard I stifle a shriek, followed by a chuckle when the speed at which we walk makes me trip once. We dash into an empty room and bang the door closed.

'What's this?' he asks after five minutes of passion, his head on my shoulder and buried in my hair. In his warm, strong hug, I can hear his heartbeat. 'A post-fight patch up?' he chuckles, his breath tickling my ear.

He holds me by the waist lightly, running his hands up and down my back and tracing my waistline, his own back to the wall. His entire body is slumped against me. I nudge his head by twitching my shoulder. When he doesn't move, I tickle him and he stands straight in a flash. Now, I chuckle and plant a kiss on his nose.

He pulls me closer, his grip growing strong. 'You bruised my lip.' He pouts to show the redness on his lower lip when I bit it seconds ago. 'Now you heal it.'

I trace my thumb over it and then rise to my feet to plant a gentle peck on his soft, parted lips. He arches a brow. 'Too gentle,' he says and starts to dive in for a passionate one when I smile against it. 'I call it love,' I whisper.

Chapter Forty

At night, after a short success party I throw for the Racketeers, I walk home tired and find Dad waiting up. His expression says he's had enough of my silence and that he is ready to talk, never mind if I am or not.

'Neha. Wait,' he calls out when I try to slink away as soon as I cross threshold. I grimace and turn around, showing very little interest in what he has to say. 'Where were you?'

'At a party.'

'Which party?'

I fail to keep a check on my sarcasm. 'It's a long story. I doubt you'd be interested, because it has nothing to do with *her*.' I look at Cecelia, who sits in the living room watching the two of us.

'That's not the answer to my question,' he says, his tone calculated to be nice but authoritative.

'We were celebrating our success.' He furrows his brows. 'I am a part of a dance group that was selected to perform at the annual function the day after tomorrow.'

His head cocks to the side. 'Dance group?' he says. 'I never knew you were interested in dancing. That's…' he searches for words, 'new.'

I shrug. 'It was more of an invitation than participation.

I was requested to join as a last resort, but now I enjoy it.'

'Wow.' He smiles with distinct pride. 'Congratulations, *beta*.'

'Congratulations. You deserved it,' Cecelia says. I look at her and frown. 'You were always a better dancer than you thought. *Million Reasons Why*, remember?'

I mutter, 'Thanks,' and smile stiffly. 'Can I go now?' I point to my room.

'Wait,' my dad says urgently. I cross my arms and lean against the door. 'You can talk to your dad now because…' he pauses. 'Well, because we're not going to marry.'

I push off from the door and stand still. They exchange glances.

It is Cecelia who breaks the silence. 'Can I talk to you for a second?' she asks me. I don't think it is appropriate to refuse. She momentarily looks at Dad who sighs and strides out.

'How do you feel now?' she asks, patting the seat next to her.

I wonder if I even feel anything. Too worn-out to think for myself, I ask her instead, 'About what?'

'About your dad not marrying me.'

'I, ah...' I thought I'd feel better, but now that I have Cecelia sitting so close to me, the same old person I spent some of my most memorable days with, I can't bring myself to say that to her face. And after all that happened in college, my patch up, our selection and all, I'm in too high spirits to hurt anyone. 'I don't know.' I settle for a safer reply.

'Why do you hate me so much?'

I blink at her. 'I don't hate you. I just don't... accept you as my mother. And frankly, I don't think anybody can ever replace her. She was, is indispensable even though she is not with us any longer.'

Cecelia places her hand on my palm. 'And who told you I was going to replace her?'

'Isn't that what you're doing? Or Dad?' I decide to get it all out now that the topic has been broached again. 'Just because she's not with us doesn't mean Dad has the right to push her out of his mind. I wonder if he even loved her as much.'

'Of course he did! I can assure you he loved your mom like he'd never loved anyone, before or after. And maybe that is why it took him twelve years to move on and get over her death.'

'I'm not over it though.'

'And no one expects you to be. But your mother's death didn't stop you from thinking about Darshak, from living your life, enjoying yourself with your friends. It's not wrong, but did you observe your father in the meantime? He cut himself off from all social gatherings and focused his energies only on you.'

I play with the hem of my knee-length peach skirt. She is right, in a way. After Mother's death, Dad had proper conversations only with me. It was always work, home, more work and back home for him.

I try to remember the last time he called one of his colleagues home or attended some office party. That was years ago. For the first five or six years after her death he didn't even smile in public. I did notice him keeping his distance, but the reason it never registered was the fact that he was always normal when he was with me.

'The only thing that kept him from going insane was you,' she continues and places the book *The Time Traveller's Wife* on the other side, narrowing the gap between us. 'When he came to Canada, he built this wall around himself and never stepped out. He opened his mouth only during presentations or while explaining something to his subordinates or to eat.

I was one of his subordinates and I observed him out of curiosity. After two years of continually talking to him and not getting anything but a slight smile or infrequent nods in return, he opened up.

I wasn't interested in him that way. I initially reached out, because I could see he needed a friend and that he was troubled, deep within. The only time I saw him break into a smile was when he spoke on that one international call he made infrequently... to you.'

I remember talking to Dad for two hours once every two or three days, while Nani pampered me with her hot, home-cooked meals. He asked me a dozen times if I was fine and how my life was going. I blabbered on about every tiny detail about my college, but never really stopped to toss the same question his way.

I bury my face in my palm, shivering as I imagine him all isolated oceans away. 'Why didn't he tell me he was hurting?'

'Because he's your dad. *He*'s supposed to be *your* strength. Not the other way round,' she says, running her hand over my hair.

'Rubbish,' I mutter through my palms.

She smiles. 'Think about it. You're his child. He has held you since you were a bald baby. For him, you'll remain that little no matter how old or mature you get. He'll instinctively want to protect you from all emotional harm. And being a father, he'd never burden you with his problems. He'll only listen to yours.'

He never put his emotions on display, but I reckon he must feel lonely sometimes. But I was too preoccupied with my own life to look back and ask him, 'Oh, by the way Dad, how was *your* day?'

What would I have done without him? I shudder at the thought. It is too unnerving to even think about.

'So what exactly are you trying to tell me?' I raise my head. 'I feel guilty now.'

'Don't. After suffering for almost ten years of his life, your dad has decided to move on and lead the life his wife, your mother, would have wanted him to.'

I scowl.

'Tell me one thing. Now that you're there for him, you can look after him. But what will happen when you're married, say, six years from now?'

What the hell! I never thought that far!

She catches the horrified look on my face. 'When you're married, engaged in adjusting to your new life, your dad will take himself out of your life. But he will be lonely. More than he is right now. And that will be the time he'll need a companion.'

I shake my head, refusing to buy her explanation.

'Firstly, he's not alone. I'm there for him. And secondly, if that's the case then I won't marry.'

'I'm asking too much of you to understand. But your dad will be happy if you do.'

'Do what?'

'Do marry and stay happy for the rest of your life. He knows he can't fend for you for all your life and he doesn't expect you to look out for him for the rest of his life. It's just how the relationships between parents and children work. It is even more complicated when the child is a girl.'

I bite my lip, trying to understand her point of view. 'I miss my mother. I'd be disloyal to her if this...'

'Who said that?' Cecelia pulls me close, her tender rose perfume having a calming effect on my nerves. 'If you think I or anyone else your dad chooses to be with will replace your mother then you're wrong. And I'm not saying this because I want you to accept me or accept our marriage. I'm just showing you the flip side. Putting forth your dad's side.

'And knowing him as well as I do, I'm sure he won't sit you down and explain it. He decided to give up on this marriage the very day you discovered the truth and acted out against it.'

I look up at her, my eyes wide and prickling. 'Did he really?'

She nods, placing her cold palm on my cheek. 'I'm not trying to save our marriage here. Before I pack my bags and board a flight to Canada tomorrow I want to clear the doubts between you two, as I am essentially the reason for them. I don't want you misjudging your dad or doubting his love for you or your mother.'

'You're leaving tomorrow?'

She doesn't say anything. I want her to stay. I wish she could attend our annual function before she leaves. And I had promised Tanna Ma'am that I'd bring Cecelia to the function.

But I have no right to ask her to hang around, since I am the reason she is leaving in the first place.

My doubts aren't cleared yet though. I decide to get candid and voice my deepest fear before I let her abandon me with a mountain of guilt and unanswered questions. 'Wouldn't people have laughed at us if he had gotten married? Or, like, doubted his character?'

The reason for my anger and refusal is not just the thought of being disloyal to Mum. It is also the fact that people would talk about my dad behind his back. And if I ever overhear someone saying anything nasty about him, I know I'll thrash them before they get a chance to snigger at their own remark.

I also know Dad would ground me if that really happens, forbidding me from seeing people at all.

'You *are* the best daughter any father could have,' she says, interrupting my violent thoughts.

'I thought I was the worst daughter he could've ever had,' I mutter and see Rocky emerge from his kennel. He stretches his front paws and walks towards his bowl, lapping at the water from the almost empty dish.

'That's utter bull,' Cecelia says and I snort. I walk to the balcony and grab a half-full bottle of water on my way. I lean against the doorframe and wait for Rocky to drink up all the water in his bowl. 'Even when you're mad at him, you're concerned about his reputation,' she adds.

'I've another word for it. Insensitive,' I say under my breath, but I'm not sure she hears me.

'He loves you more than he ever loved me or even your mother. He'll never do anything that'd make you sad.'

Rocky wags his tail when I sit beside him and pour water into his bowl. He pokes his head out from under my armpit. I loop my arm around his neck to hold him back.

Am I keeping Dad from smiling? What about the troubles we would face after he ties the knot at this age? But his happiness…

'I think I've told you all I want to,' Cecelia says through the balcony door, watching us from a distance. Rocky does not turn to look at her. He had learnt early on to let Cecelia be.

Initially, he barked his head off whenever she barged into the living room. But now neither of them acknowledges the other. They've adopted the mantra live and let live.

'All the best for your dance, Neha. And for your career and life in general. I think it's safe to say I'll miss you.'

She is talking as if she is fleeing this very instant. I toss her a look over my shoulder, my eyes narrowing. 'You will be in touch, won't you?'

She fidgets with the jacket of the book in her hand. 'I doubt that's a great idea.'

For a moment, I imagine the house without her, empty; no accented voice ricocheting off the walls; no clinking of knives and forks; no fights with the housemaid; no one to open the door when I return tired from college; no one to share my crazy stories with; no one who'd ask me if I had had a tiff with my boyfriend; no one who'd pass expert, mature judgments on how I looked each day.

In a month I've gotten used to her presence more than I would like to admit. And there is no denying I'd miss her presence at least for the next few days.

There is also no denying that Dad and she are, in our words, breaking up. And the prime rule of getting over anyone is to cease all contact with that person. Sometimes, with all the people associated with them till you're over it.

I fondle Rocksy's bushy coat before using him to push myself to my feet. When I face Cecelia, in a blue jumpsuit gazing at me with kind eyes, I drop the bottle beside the balcony railing and embrace her. She squeezes me back, inviting resentful barks from Rocky.

I didn't realize I missed having someone around until she came. And whether I like to admit it or not, I'd miss that again.

Chapter Forty-One

'Neha?' A soft hand brushes my hair. I strain my eyes to see a plump figure standing near my bed, knees touching the mattress and the other hand resting on the headboard. I stir and shoot up in my bed to see light swelling around me. I squint to see the face through the beams of light. 'How are you?'

'Mummy?' I whisper, my back bathed in sweat.

'Yes.'

I sniffle, my breath coming out in short gasps. I writhe under the blanket, fling it down and stretch out to reach her. When I can't feel any mass, can only see heaps of brightness, I cry. 'I miss you.'

'I know,' I hear the voice, which is so much like wind chimes. Just like the one I recall from my earliest memory. 'I'm here.'

'Please come back. I want you!' I say, now sure it is her. 'Come back!' I wail every word into the light, not convinced that she can hear me.

A violent shake on my arm wakes me up with a start. I find Cecelia ordering me to open my eyes. She pulls the blanket off me and grips my arms.

'I'm here,' she says, her skin cold and eyes red, sleep deprived. She puts the AC on. When she settles on my bed, my mind comes out of its daze. I hug her and bury my face in her soft night suit.

My bed is soaked with sweat and tears trickle down my cheek. I feel my heart squeeze. I cry again, saying words like, 'I want her back', and 'I miss her' and Cecelia pulls me into a tighter hug, muffling my voice. Before I know it, my breath evens out and I slip into sleep when the room and my body cool down.

I wake up in the morning to a squawking alarm and find myself wound up in a hot blanket. The room is chilled and fog obscures the windows. I find Cecelia sleeping on one of the chairs at my desk, her head resting on the computer table.

* * *

The day before the function, there is an absolute hustle and bustle in college. There are no lectures and every soul in college seems caught up in doing something. Nobody has the time to stop and chat.

Darshak is busy with his rehearsals. I haven't been there for almost two weeks now. I've missed their progress. By what Darshak tells me, they're absolutely ready to take the stage.

My dance group has decided to take this day off. We don't practice and simply help the faculty put up the stage, decorate and decide on what to gift our chief guests, winning teams, participants, deserving staff members and toppers. Youngsters think our function is a good place to showcase their talents, so we make sure we stand up to that reputation. We're also known for welcoming guests from diverse fields and not just the conventional, famous faces.

While I'm busy counting the certificates and stamping them with our college seal, Tanna Ma'am approaches me. 'Cecelia is coming to the function, isn't she?' she asks, pulling the phone away from her ear. 'Rachael Biswas has asked if she would be present. And I said yes.'

I hesitate, my eyes widening. Ma'am waits for the answer she wants to hear. 'Yeah.'

'Good.' As if she had never been expecting another reply, she returns to the call. I'm frozen in place. 'Oh. And another thing.' She whirls around and I straighten like a military cadet in front of his commanding officer. 'When she arrives, request her to meet me in my cabin. She will hand the bouquet to Mrs Biswas.'

I nod stiffly and watch her stride off with a small smile directed my way… which might turn into a scowl when she learns the truth.

* * *

When I carry the costumes to the dance room, still looking for ways to cook up a story for Cecelia's absence, I hear Ritesh, Darshak and Shreya murmuring to each other. The word 'Cecelia' catches my attention. I tip-toe into the room, dump our costumes there and hide behind a classroom door to listen to them.

'She *said* she's not coming tomorrow.' This is Darshak. He sounds annoyed.

'But she freaking has to! She can't just choreograph our dance, get us all emotionally attached to her, see her discipline the crap out of us so we give our best performance, pep talk us into believing in ourselves and then disappear like she never existed!' Is that Ritesh? I've seen him get angry a lot of times before. But this is a different kind of anger. And what was that about choreography?

Shreya's timid voice follows. 'There's nothing we can really do, is there?'

'No!' Ritesh snaps, his temple looking like it's throbbing. He makes an attempt to move away. 'I'll go get her.'

'Have you lost it?' Darshak grabs Ritesh's shirt firmly. He seems to be losing it too. They stare each other down for a moment before Darshak sighs and leans against the wall, gazing at his shoes. 'There's a personal problem she's facing right now. I have vowed not to tell on her. But trust me, it is a reason serious enough that she can't make it.'

My breath is caught in my throat, eyes wide in horror. He *knows*.

'I won't perform unless she's there.'

Shreya squeaks. 'Don't do that!'

'If not for her, Shreya, we'd be sitting in the audience tomorrow clapping for others and having to bear those snickers behind our backs. You know how they talk about us. Or do I need to remind you?' The sadness in his voice is hard to miss even under all that anger.

'She won't like it if you opt out at the last moment, bro. Seriously, don't do that,' Darshak says.

'What if we tell Neha everything? Can't she just do something about it?' Shreya asks. I shift the weight on my leg. I've lost count of the number of people I've disappointed.

'No. Cecelia has firmly warned us against that.'

'But why?'

'She doesn't want Neha to feel obliged and then accountable to her for her actions,' Darshak explains.

'What actions?'

'That's none of our business. I reckon we should simply respect her decision.'

'*I* won't,' Ritesh snaps. 'I won't perform tomorrow if she doesn't come. I don't care what her problems are. But if she can do so much for us already, she can certainly come to wish us one last time.'

Why is he so obsessed with Cecelia?

Before either of them can persuade him, Ritesh storms off; Shreya rushing after him and Darshak staring at them with a tired look on his face.

Chapter Forty-Two

'None of our business, huh?'

Darshak turns at the sound of my voice and freezes in place, caught unawares. 'Neha? When did you...'

'What was that?'

'Wh...what?'

'I heard everything.' I nod in the direction Ritesh and Shreya left. 'What were you talking about?'

He hesitates, chewing his lip as if debating whether to tell me or not.

My eyes soften. 'Please, Darshak. I get enough guilt from everywhere. I am the reason my dad, Cecelia, Tanna Ma'am, you and now even my dance group apparently are or will be unhappy. Please.'

I close the distance between us and stand in front of him. He takes my arm, gently but firmly and pulls me into the dance room. 'What do you want to know?' he asks sitting me down on a chair and taking a seat next to me.

'Everything. What was that conversation about? Why didn't anybody tell me Cecelia was involved in choreographing our dance? How come you talked as if you knew what Cecelia's problem was?'

'Because I do know what her problem is.'

I wait for him to say more.

'Okay, listen. When you didn't pick up my calls those four days pretending you were not well, I called Cecelia. Don't ask me how I got her number. We exchanged it at the theatre. She told me if I ever needed to reach you but couldn't, I could call her any time. I wasn't flirting or anything, don't misinterpret it.'

'I know that,' I say impatiently, rolling my eyes. 'Cut to the chase.'

'I called her and she said you were upset. I asked the reason but she wouldn't answer, saying it wasn't her story to tell. I begged and told her I wouldn't speak of it to a soul. It sounded dramatic but I meant it. So she told me.'

I narrow my eyes. 'What exactly did she tell you?'

'About what happened that day; the truth about your father and her, your reaction to it and the events that followed. She sounded sad but composed. I figured this must've been the reason you lashed out at me the other day. But what hurt me the most was that you, of all people, didn't feel confident enough to confide in me.'

I stir in my seat, noticeably ill at ease and self-conscious. What is this? Make-Neha-feel-guilty month? 'I'm sorry,' I mumble.

He squeezes my hands. 'I'm not blaming you. Just saying. I could imagine what you have been going through.' I smile. 'After she was done, I asked her whether she could choreograph your dance. One last favour. I knew you wouldn't ask, now that you hated her more than you ever did before, so I did.'

I grimace at that. I never hated her, but if that was what was being conveyed through my actions then I sincerely needed to apologize.

'She agreed on one condition. That you would never find out she was involved in this. I promised her. When I told your dance group to keep it a secret too, they were more than keen to do that. They were so desperate for a tutor that they would have chopped their arms off if she had asked them too.'

Talk about exaggeration.

But now things fall into place. Shreya was never a great liar. That explained all her nervousness the other day when she asked me to be a member of her group. She wasn't scared of me, but worried about pulling off the act and hiding the truth.

Darshak continues, 'In the following days, Cecelia came and trained them. I used to take her to and from college.'

Every morning she was out jogging and attending office. Is this what her 'jogging' had been?

I've not yet recovered from the shock when I hear Darshak's words. 'Being the quick learners that they are, your group grasped her steps within a week. That was when the group developed a bond with her. She wasn't merely a tutor, she instilled faith in them.

'She was like a pillar. She was also the only one who trusted in your abilities. You should have seen them learn. It was priceless. Her pep talk was carried forward to you when you joined them later.'

I know how her teaching must have felt. She is a good teacher and when she taught me, learning came very easily. It is the confidence that she instils in every cell of your body that makes it easy to rely on her.

And now I know why she opted to talk to me the day

before. She supposed I'd be in a decent frame of mind, what with our win, and so would be less hurtful to her. I never knew she thought about me so much. I'm flattered in a way.

'I called her last night to make sure she was coming for the big show. But when she said she was leaving today, I was shocked. But not as much as Ritesh, who is more attached to her than any of us. He apparently survived his parent's divorce because of her.'

Ritesh.

I'm suddenly immobilized in my seat. I pull out my phone and scroll through my contact list in a daze. I find Ritesh's phone number and stare at it for what seems like eternity. It looks so familiar, much like the one I saw calling Cecelia's iPhone the other day.

Oh god, yes. He was the one calling her from his phone. Since she couldn't talk to him in front of me, she left the house each time she had to take it. And she left the house to attend unknown calls a lot.

I close my eyes to let it all sink in. I don't register that Darshak has wrapped his arm around my shoulder. All I can think of right now is what I've done.

It seems like an unstated fact. Apart from me, not a single person who has bumped into her wants her to leave. Suddenly, I feel like a twisted, evil soul who is only concerned about herself. Purti's words ring in my ears. I really *am* a self-centred person.

Sure, I don't fancy Cecelia's departure. Otherwise, I wouldn't have felt bad for a second while she announced the news.

But Cecelia is the reason Dad is back to normal, smiling

like he used to in all those pictures when Mom was alive. She is the reason I am considered more important in college and in the eyes of the teachers, more than I deserve. She is the reason a misjudged but worthy group of students is realizing their potential and believes in themselves again. She has lent me a hand in ways I can't even begin to list.

And she had done all that even when she knew I didn't want her in my life.

'Neha...' Darshak calls out. I look at him and see his eyes searching my face. 'You okay?'

The concern in his voice squeezes my heart. I don't know how I survived the last two weeks without talking to Darshak at all. I've been so used to him that I have started to take his presence in my life for granted, assuming he'll always be there to comfort me when I'm nothing but a messy puddle.

What if he's taken away from me in the blink of an eye? Without warning, without explanation. The thought of losing him seems nauseating and nightmarish. And I'm expecting Dad and Cecelia to live that nightmare.

'Neha! What's wrong?' He gives my arm a shake.

I cup Darshak's face in my hands. I look at him, taking mental pictures of the lines around his eyes, his face, and lean forward to kiss him full on the lips.

His muscles tense and he doesn't kiss me back immediately, but then eases into it. His arms gingerly reach my back and I pull him closer. The kiss isn't passionate, but it's urgent and reeks of desperation at my end.

When I pull back, I brush my thumb across his cheek and reflect his concerned look with a smile.

'Thank you,' I say.

Without stopping to explain where I'm going, I sprint out of college and take a cab to my house hoping against hope I'd find her home and that I'm not too late in realizing what I'm about to lose.

Chapter Forty-Three

When I reach home, Dad isn't there. That means Cecelia won't be leaving for a few more hours. She unlocks the door and is surprised to find me standing there, panting and wheezing as if I've run a marathon. It is too early for me to be back. I had told her I'd be at college all day.

She hands me a glass of water and asks if I want tea or coffee. I shake my head while drinking the water. She then excuses herself saying she has to pack, her voice distant and shaky. Had she been crying before I walked in?

I panic at the thought. This is the second time I've made her cry in a month. I dump my bag on the kitchen table and dash into her bedroom unannounced.

'Don't go,' I say without preamble. She turns and cocks her head to the side. 'I mean you're needed at the function. I promised Tanna Ma'am you'll be there. You can go the day after.'

What has gotten into me? I'm supposed to plead for her not to go back to Canada. Not order her to stay for a few more days, so she can meet my selfish needs.

'I'd have loved to, but I can't reschedule my flight, can I? I am not that influential yet.' She smiles, tugging the jeans on her waist slightly so she can fit into it. 'I'll write an apology note to your teacher explaining why I can't make it, if you want.'

I nod slowly, unsure what to say next. She resumes loading her blue bag with neatly folded summer dresses. I stroll inside and sit on one end of her bed and watch her as she works.

'Why did you come here?' I ask her. I know the meeting was only one of the reasons… or probably, an excuse.

'I guess to try and fit into your father's world?' she admits. 'To see if I could adjust to the life he leads, whether I could get along well with you. Because, by and large, loving someone is not enough. And people tend to get a little more cautious before making decisions when they are as old as your dad is or as I am. They don't act on impulse like most young people do.'

'Do you really, like, love my dad? As in, as much as I love Darshak or my mom loved him?'

She pauses for a few seconds before answering. 'I don't think what I feel for your dad can be compared with either. With you and Darshak, you don't worry if his family will accept you. Because frankly, you both are too young to think about it. You love to be together and for now, that's all that matters.

'In your father's case, your parents were first bonded by law. There was no question of acceptance, since the only acceptance that was needed in their relationship was each other's. Eventually, as they built a life together, they grew to love each other.'

'Then what is it in your case?' I cross my legs into a lotus position ready to hear her story.

'I think we both connected primarily out of need. What bonded us was the fact that both of us were alone. We took it one day at a time, pushing forward in the darkness as the days stretched on.

'Though I had my family to fall back on after my divorce and your dad had you, it somehow wasn't enough. We could only talk about our problems to our families, not share them. When the two of us chatted over a period of time, the realization dawned on us that we aren't alone in what felt like loneliness. I felt like I belonged.' She dumps her shoe box into the bag, pressing it to zip it closed. She heaves a sigh and looks at me.

'The most powerful feeling that can get you through anything in life is the feeling of belongingness. The belief that you belong to someone, that your absence will be felt, is what keeps you going every day. You need to have that someone in your life. Back there, for your father, that person was me. And for me, it was him.'

I ponder over her words. I hope I don't sound too nosy when I ask what I do. 'Did he, I mean did Dad propose to you? As in with a ring and all like they show in the movies?' I never expected to be questioning my dad's lover; I always thought it'd be the other way round. Though it is less of an interrogation and more of a curiosity satisfaction thing.

I'm determined to identify with his situation, get to the crux of it before I punish him for no fault of his own. I know I couldn't stay away from Darshak if I was asked to and so I have no right to make someone else suffer. Just because Dad has voluntarily given me the right to decide for him, doesn't mean I do if it's not in his best interest.

I don't want him to stay behind the walls he's created around himself forever. It is my duty as his only child to pull him out of it, no matter how much he willingly locks himself in for his kid.

Cecelia scoffs at my question. She heaves the bag on the floor and sits on the bed next to me. 'Not officially,' she says. 'When you grow up, how you propose or convey your love is of little significance. What matters is whether you smile when you're with the person; whether you feel like a weight has been lifted from your shoulders; whether you feel liberated and like you belong.'

'Did you? Feel all that I mean.'

She inhales. 'I guess so. We initially mostly shared our sorrows, not joys. We'd both found a person with whom we could share and just be ourselves. It didn't feel weird to talk about silly things with your dad and still have the confidence that I was accepted and respected all the same.' I grin, for the first time being able to relate to what she says. 'But why are you asking all this?'

I hesitate. Should I say it now? 'Because… I… I like you.' That didn't come out right.

'I know that.' She tucks a strand of my hair behind my ear and smiles. 'And I like you.'

'No. I mean, I would like to have you as my mother.'

She stares at me with a frown between her eyebrows, as if the news doesn't surprise her. 'But?' she asks.

God, she can read my mind.

'I… I'm worried what people will say. And also, I'm not being disloyal to my mother by accepting you.' I look up at the ceiling and back at Cecelia. 'And I want *her* to know that.'

'Why did you ever feel I was aiming to take your mother's place? Or your father's wife's place for that matter.'

'You aren't?' I ask her, a little dazed.

She shakes her head. 'I will always be, whether I admit it or not, his third love. That is after you and your mother. I always aimed at being your friend first. I never intended to replace her. In fact, I don't want to. I just want to be a part of your lives, be a friend to you and a companion to your dad in his old age.'

'Oh.' That is all I could manage.

'And if you doubt whether I'll be able to keep your father happy, then just rewind a month of your life. I had never seen him so happy than when the two of us were having a good time together. Did you see his face? I have never seen him so content or relaxed, even back in Canada.'

I think about it for a minute. 'Neither have I.' She waits for me to say something. 'If I ask you to marry my dad, will you? I mean, I don't want him to sacrifice a second chance at love for me. I'm not that cruel, you know.'

She chuckles. 'You never were, my dear.'

I'm grateful she feels that way.

She runs her hand through my hair. 'You're still worried about what people will say, aren't you?'

I fall silent. Yes, I'm worried. But I could handle those stares for my dad. The only person whose reaction I was scared about was Darshak, but he has apparently accepted Cecelia… even before I did.

'Maybe,' I say. 'But what others say is none of our concern. Your happiness is what I want. And what I want is already mine.'

I lock her into a gentle embrace that lifts a thousand pound weight off my heart. She cradles me for some time and it feels like I have finally done the right thing.

Chapter Forty-Four

'Dad.' I open the door to him and fling my arms around his round belly. He jerks at the sudden display of affection, but then hugs me back with a quick squeeze, his chin resting on my head. Cecelia strides out from her bedroom. When their eyes lock, she gives him a withdrawn smile.

'Are you done packing?' he asks her, his voice casual, void of any emotion. Cecelia shrugs. I had warned her against saying anything and had asked her to play along.

'When are we leaving?'

He narrows his eyes at me when we pull away from each other. 'We?'

'Of course! What did you think? I wouldn't want to come to drop off one of my best friends?'

He peeks at Cecelia as she fights a smile. She struggles to keep her face straight. He glances down at his watch and then at me. 'In two hours.'

'Hmmm,' I say, taking the suitcase from his hand and ushering him into a chair. 'Did you buy any souvenirs for her?'

He stares at me, his face confused. Maybe he's wondering why his daughter is abruptly being pleasant to the person she hates, or just being pleasant in general.

'What? Don't tell me you didn't get her anything. Your

future wife is going to Canada and you didn't buy her stuff she could flaunt in front of her friends?' He eyes me, still not comprehending the situation. I dump his bag on the table, sit on a chair next to him and muster up a sincere expression. 'I agree to your marriage, Papa. I want Cecelia in our lives. I accept her.'

He shoots us looks, trying to gauge any signs of sarcasm. 'Is this…?'

'I'm not kidding. Now please sell that plane ticket, because she's coming to my show tomorrow. If she doesn't then, well, I'll reconsider giving my consent.'

Dad blinks, then his confused look turns into disbelief and finally into a smile. I edge closer to him and look into his old, kind eyes. I hadn't noticed how dark and hollow they had become with age. 'And I'm sorry… for mistrusting you, for being so mean.' I press his warm hands between mine. 'For everything. You didn't deserve it after you've been the best father.'

He kisses my forehead, trying to convey his sentiments through the gesture and strolls over to Cecelia to pull her into a hug. Cecelia mouths, 'Thank you,' to me over his shoulder before closing her eyes in his embrace.

I smile.

Chapter Forty-Five

Not only am *I* thrilled to have Cecelia back, but Tanna Ma'am, Darshak, my dance group and even Rachael Biswas Ma'am look pleased. Relief washes over Tanna Ma'am's face when she sees Cecelia. They apparently already know each other—what with Cecelia attending college every day to teach us.

Ritesh is the person who is always by her side talking and smiling a lot for the first time. I never realized they had grown so close.

Dad takes half a day off and graces our annual function with his presence for a couple of hours.

We get into our costumes and brace for the final performance. Before we can go on stage, Cecelia gives us a piece of advice. 'Dance because you want to. Not because you have to.'

When Shreya asks me later whether I'd like to be a permanent part of the Racketeers, I don't hesitate to say yes. More than I trust my own dance skills, I trust Cecelia's teaching. And the best part is I won't have to go out looking for a dance tutor to be formally trained.

* * *

When I'm done with my dance, I come backstage to roaring cheers. Everyone's congratulating Shreya and

Ritesh. I get pats on the back from my friends and Darshak practically lifts me in the air the moment he sees me. That is when I see Purti standing a few feet away, smiling. I excuse myself from the crowd and go up to her.

'That was good,' she tells me, swirling hot water around in her bottle. She drinks it before every performance.

'Thanks…' I start and stare at her, my voice caught in my throat. I have missed her. We're both quiet for some time before I throw my hands around her neck. She spills her water on my back and I wince, but don't let her go. 'I'm sorry.'

'No!' she says, holding me at arm's length. '*I'm* sorry. That's what I wanted to tell you. I was waiting for your performance to end.'

She takes my arm and pulls me to a quieter corner. She explains that she knew everything about me. At the trek when Purti couldn't shut up about how much she hated me, Cecelia had made her understand what I was going through. They had had a heart-to-heart talk and since I had been their topic of discussion, they shut up every time I passed by.

Great. I had spent this entire time thinking Purti was sharing her heartbreak, but now I know she was being told what a selfish ass I was.

But it looks like Cecelia hadn't told her how selfish I was. She, in fact, told Purti I was a friend for life, someone who would take a bullet for her people and would never hurt them on purpose. All that, when I had made it obvious that I had wanted her out of my life.

For a second I close my eyes, thinking again how lucky I am to have her. Cecelia had also given Purti strength saying that if she could find love at the age of forty-two, then sooner or later Purti will find love too.

'She is good at that,' Purti smiles, looking at Cecelia standing a few feet away. 'Giving people strength.' I mirror her smile. Who knows that better than I do? 'And I'm really sorry for waiting so long to tell you this. I really didn't want to...'

'It's okay,' I say, not wanting to prolong this discussion. It's a good day and it's been a great start. 'I have something for you,' I tell her and pull out a bottle of honey from my bag. I take a spoonful and force feed it to her, something I do before every show of hers. It's like a tradition. 'Go burn up the stage,' I smile and see her eyes well up.

'Thanks, love.'

* * *

I cheer them on from behind the curtains during the band's performances, giving a thumbs-up whenever Darshak glances sideways. They conclude their last performance with a song called, *I'm Here For You* by the Game Players. It is really a song about friendship, but if you twist around a few words it could be about love.

'They're really a good team,' Cecelia says beside me. I look at her, her face as bright as the sun. She's wearing a simple blue saree and holding a golden box clutch.

Since we arrived in college together I've been running around like a headless chicken, doing ten things at the same time. Now that my dance is done and the band is on stage, their performance being the last for tonight, I can finally be with her.

Not that she is bored without me. She was treated like

a mini-celebrity by Tanna Ma'am and especially Ritesh. I haven't seen her without at least one of the members of my dance group by her side. She was either with them or Rachael Biswas or Rachael's daughter, who had accompanied her mother to our function. They've all been taking good care of her.

'Better than us?' I ask Cecelia, wrapping my arm around her elbow.

She pretends to think. Then smiles. 'Nay. We're a team for life.'

I snort and rest my head on her shoulder. She runs her thick, long fingers across my cheek, making me aware of how much I've gained in the last one month with the arrival of just one guest. A guest who's here to stay.

Acknowledgements

I'd like to express my gratitude to all those without whom this book wouldn't have been possible:

First and above all, my mentor and publisher, Ravin Sir, who showed faith in my writing and led me to the end of the tunnel. He's kind with criticism, generous with compliments, incredibly patient and supportive. His expert character study and understanding of the story, along with valuable suggestions and inputs based on them, inspired me to work harder. I knew my debut novel was in the right hands. Thank you for letting me have the last word in during the editorial process, and for not giving up on the script even as I changed the tense of the whole book halfway through the rewriting process. In essence, thank you for standing by new authors.

My dad, who is more excited than I am about this book's release. Thank you for making me a book lover and for being my first reader. I wouldn't have found my passion if it wasn't for you. I'm a part of you, and that will always echo through my name.

My mom, for standing back and letting me stay up at night; for making sure I was well fed and okay while I wrote. You have seen me at my worst and my best while writing. Thank you for also patiently putting up with my rants over characters and plots.

In a time when parents would usually utter words of shock if their daughter tells them she wants to be a writer, you two are the ones jumping in jubilation and announcing it proudly.

My sister, Chaitali. She's a forced reader, but a very valuable critique. Also, without her, I would never know what suffocating feels like. Your hugs are going to kill someone some day. But thank you, every writer needs it. I mean your honest opinions, not the hugs.

My Kelkar, Ruia and Mithibai College friends. Thank you for making my college life enjoyable and thank you for all the memories that will keep popping up directly or indirectly in my writing.

I would also like to thank my Ruia and Mithibai teachers from the literature department. Grazilia and Manoj Khatri from *Complete Wellbeing* for introducing me to the other side of publishing.

Neha, my friend, for letting me borrow her name. It was supposed to be the protagonist's temporary name, but it just stuck with her until the end.

Sachin Vaidya Kaka, for always being there—just a phone call away. Genelia and Riteish Deshmukh, for being generous and allowing me to retain their names. It means a lot to me.

The team of editors, proofreaders and illustrators at Black Ink Books. You're the reason this book has turned out the way it has. Thank you, Sabine, for the heartening words and your expert eye. I feel lucky to be a part of a publication where newcomers are welcomed, cherished and revered so much.

The many others, who may not have contributed to this book, but to my life, which has ultimately enriched my work.

And last but not the least, thank you, dear reader, for buying or borrowing this book; for spending the time and money to read and share the words I've written. You are the reason books and writers continue to thrive.